FINDING THE VEIN

FINDING THE VEIN

Jennifer Hanlon Wilde

Ooligan Press · Portland, Oregon

Finding the Vein
© 2021 Jennifer Hanlon Wilde

ISBN13: 978-1-947845-24-4

Ooligan Press
Portland State University
Post Office Box 751, Portland, Oregon 97207
503.725.9748
ooligan@ooliganpress.pdx.edu
http://ooligan.pdx.edu

Library of Congress Cataloging-in-Publication Data
Names: Wilde, Jennifer Hanlon, 1969- author.
Title: Finding the vein / Jennifer Hanlon Wilde.
Description: Portland, Oregon : Ooligan Press, Portland State University, 2021
Series: Ooligan Press Library Writers Project Collection
Identifiers: LCCN 2020039417 (print) | LCCN 2020039418 (ebook) |
ISBN 9781947845244 (trade paperback) | ISBN 9781947845251 (ebook)
Classification: LCC PS3558.U323 F56 2021 (print) | LCC PS3558.U323
(ebook) | DDC 813/.54--dc23
LC record available at https://lccn.loc.gov/2020039417
LC ebook record available at https://lccn.loc.gov/2020039418

Cover design by Des Hewson
Interior design and illustrations by Bailey Potter

References to website URLs were accurate at the time of writing. Neither the author nor Ooligan Press is responsible for URLs that have changed or expired since the manuscript was prepared.

Printed in the United States of America

Library Writers Project

Ooligan Press and Multnomah County Library have created a unique partnership celebrating the Portland area's local authors. Each fall since 2015, Multnomah County Library has solicited submissions of self-published works of fiction by local authors to be added to its Library Writers Project ebook collection. Multnomah County Library and Ooligan Press have partnered to bring these previously ebook-only works to print. *Finding the Vein* is the third in an annual series of Library Writers Project books to be published by Ooligan Press. To learn more about the Library Writers Project, visit https://multcolib.org/library-writers-project.

Ooligan Press Library Writers Project Collection

Finding the Vein by Jennifer Hanlon Wilde (2021)
Iditarod Nights by Cindy Hiday (2020)
The Gifts We Keep by Katie Grindeland (2019)

This book is dedicated to the foster families and social workers of Holt Sahathai, whose unswerving dedication to the children in their care makes all the difference.

PROLOGUE

July 25, 10:30 p.m.

The scent of burnt marshmallows rose in the night air. The sky was growing dark and the campers' laughter was turning shrill and hysterical. Late nights and sugar got them seriously wound up, but that was half the fun of Heritage Camp. Paul Anderson accepted his third pie in the face with a good-natured smile, even though he thought his friend Katie planted it quite a bit harder than she needed to. He rubbed his nose and laughed, but she didn't laugh with him. She just smirked, her eyes glittering in the light from the campfire.

Paul licked the whipped cream off his face and grinned as though it were delicious. In fact, it tasted like OFF! Deep Woods spray, and his tongue went numb.

"Have mercy, Nathan. Use the lifeline next time," he said, speaking to a chubby boy with bushy hair and glasses. They stood together on a small platform at the edge of the woods, in front of a large campfire ringed with stones. A group of about ninety campers of all ages sat—and bounced and giggled and fidgeted—on wooden benches arranged like the seats in an amphitheater, watching the game unfold. Most of the kids were Asian, like him, though a few were from Ethiopia or Haiti. Some, like his friend Hal, were mixed race. Where they were from didn't matter; what they all had in common was adoption. And despite the usual camp quarrels and dramas, they loved being together with other kids who knew what that was like: to feel different from their families, to be picked on at school, to have a blank space where other people had baby pictures. Despite everything he'd been through, Paul loved camp too.

"I'll get the next one right," Nathan promised.

"Yo Heritage Camp!" Ty hollered from his wheelchair. He was a round-faced young man with a booming voice, clever eyes, and a black fauxhawk. He always ran Heritage Trivia gleefully, appearing to relish his role as game-show host.

"Yo what!" the campers shouted as one.

"Are we ready for the next question? Which counselors! Are! From! China!"

Nathan appeared to think deeply. "Hmm. Jia? Molly. And Paul?"

"I'm calling hacks!" Paul cried. "He got that wrong on purpose!"

"Are you playing your one and only switch card, brother Paul?" Ty shouted.

"Yes I am, brother Ty. Switch, please."

Ty said, "Then the question goes to Annie. Remember, campers get to answer the questions, but the counselors get the pies!"

A girl with pink hair smiled widely, showing her braces. "That would be Xia, not Jia. Molly is correct. And Alex, not Paul—he's from Thailand."

"That is correct! Switch card means...the correct answer gets the pie! Get her, Paul!" Ty shouted.

Katie's mouth dropped open. "What?!"

The campers broke into applause as Paul accepted the pie, and they screamed with laughter as he planted it in Katie's face.

After the trivia and the campfire songs, the mail was distributed and the campers were quiet for a short time, reading their letters or gazing at their friends' mail rather than their own empty hands. Paul washed his face off in the lake and played a medley of pop songs on his clarinet.

When he was finished, Ty announced, "Adoptees Got Talent is over, ladies and gentlemen!"

"But what about ghost stories?" a little girl asked. Paul recognized little Eliza, attired in her usual outfit: shorts, a T-shirt, and fairy wings. The wings were growing floppy and ragged.

"No ghost stories, Tinkerbell—not on my watch. Under-twelves to your cabins; everyone else to the lodge for the dance party at eleven! Stay with your buddy!" Very quickly, the campers began to disperse and head up the path. Their noisy procession was a medley of bright sweatshirts, ponytails, sandals, and sleek, otter-brown heads. Paul coughed.

The camp nurse—a tall, thin woman with blond hair who stood out in the crowd—hung back. "Paul? Are you okay?"

"Yeah. Thanks, Genevieve. It's just the wood smoke—it bothers me sometimes."

"I'll be at the lodge doing night meds," she said. "In case you need me."

"Thanks," he said, relieved; she didn't seem mad at him at all. She turned to Sophie, looking slightly worried. She always looked that way when speaking to her daughter. Paul had noticed it before.

"Aren't you coming up, Sophie?" she asked.

"I'll be there in a minute."

"Don't dilly-dally, sweetheart."

"Mom."

Genevieve looked reluctant to go. But a small voice from up the path called, "Nurse? We need some first aid here!" and she hurried away, glancing back. Sophie rolled her eyes—they were green today—and smiled at Paul.

Paul disassembled his clarinet and stowed it, snapping the case shut as the counselors in training (CITs) doused the campfire and then chased each other up the path, hurling marshmallows and laughing. One grazed Paul's ear. He picked it up and fired it, popping it neatly off the back of Nathan's retreating head.

Sophie stepped close to him as he stood up. "I like that song you played." She sang the melody quietly. She was off-key and he suppressed a smile.

"Miley Cyrus," he said lightly, stepping back. "Why do people like pop music?"

She stepped closer again. "It helps them with their feelings. The ones they don't know how to say out loud."

"Sophie." He should move away. He didn't.

"Paul," she said, gently mocking. "No one is watching." She put her hand on the back of his neck and kissed him. To reach, she had to stand on tiptoe, which meant balancing on one leg while the other—the prosthetic one—rested on its toes slightly behind her. The position was awkward, and it canted her forward slightly, so that he thought she was falling and reached out to steady her, dropping his clarinet case. But she was not falling; she was used to the imbalance. When he reached for her she reached back, and they were suddenly pressed together, which felt amazing and was exactly what he had tried to avoid, even as the heat gathered in his stupid, stupid body that didn't care about the rules. There were several reasons why kissing her was not okay. *But she started it*, his body argued. Her mouth was soft and her hair smelled like flowers along with smoke and burnt marshmallows. Then he heard a little noise in the woods. Was it a twig snapping? Or just a bird? He squinted into the darkness and thought for a second he saw a green T-shirt moving through the trees. *The CITs wore green*. It jolted him back to reality. He put a hand on her shoulder and stepped back.

"Sophie. I don't want to be that guy."

"Is it about the video?" she asked, looking down. "I told you, I don't do that anymore. Why are you being so..."

He hoped she wouldn't say what Ty had said: *so fucking good all the time*. People seemed to think that. He wished it were true.

"I know that. I'm not judging you, Sophie." He spoke quickly to stop her from saying it. "And I deleted it. I told him to do the same thing."

"Is that what you two were arguing about?"

"No, it's—look, it doesn't matter." He took another step back, and tried to focus on the crunch of the pine needles, the scent of smoke in the air, anything but Sophie's puzzled and yearning expression. He told himself, probably for the thousandth time, that he was doing the best thing. "I'm leaving my phone anyway, when I go."

"Seriously? You're still planning to go?"

"Yeah, Sophie." He tried to say it gently. "I am."

Now she was the one to step back. Her face turned hard and angry. "It's so stupid. This was Tanya's idea, wasn't it?"

"No," he said, frustrated. "It's about me. Nobody else has to understand." Which was a good thing, he thought, since nobody did, apart from Tanya. But he didn't want to think about Tanya now, either.

"Let's go up, okay?" he said. "I need my inhaler." He coughed again, feeling the slight wheeze from the smoke.

Their flip-flops slapped the dark path that wound through the woods, past the darkened infirmary and the younger kids' cabins. As they approached the lodge, a huge log building, they moved apart. The air pulsed with the thump of the bass line as dance music emanated from the lodge. Suddenly Paul wanted to dance with Sophie. It would be okay just to dance. He didn't really want anyone else to put their arms around her, smell her flowery shampoo, feel her little breasts pressed against them. He wanted that off-kilter feeling as she moved into him, just one last time. He opened the door for her and then propelled her to the dance floor under the pulsating lights. Someone had obtained a disco ball and hung it from a beam overhead.

"What about your inhaler?"

"It can wait," he said. Feeling breathless and a little dizzy, he spoke quietly into her ear. "Some things can wait."

At that, she gave him a tremulous smile. But then she frowned and said, "Are you okay? You look puffy."

"I'm fine," he said. But even as he spoke, he knew he wasn't. His throat felt tight, his chest raw and itchy. "I could use a Benadryl," he said. A small whistle escaped him as he spoke. "Get your mom—*whee*—my inhaler—*whee*—" Now the feeling was congealing in his neck. It felt like a panic attack, like he used to have before a party or a presentation at school, but he knew this was different: his lips and eyelids were swelling, and the feeling was spreading inside his chest. *Fuck, this hadn't happened in years*, he had been so careful! He fumbled for his EpiPen in his pocket, got it out of its case, and tried to steady his hand as he shoved it into his right thigh.

"Paul? Let's go sit down!" Sophie was shouting over the music, pulling on his arm.

"Okay," he tried to say, but his voice wasn't working. Only a rasping noise came out. His heart was racing and his fingers trembled. The EpiPen fell to the floor and he patted his pockets, his hands seeking his inhaler. But it wasn't there. He hardly ever needed it, so he'd stopped carrying it around—he could picture it in his toiletry bag. He could only mouth the words at Sophie's horrified face: *my inhaler*. He made no noise, not even a thump as he hit the floor—the music was too loud—but he heard Sophie clearly screaming "MOM!" It was a few long seconds before the nurse arrived, pulling the yellow canister from her fanny pack as she ran to him, opening it with her teeth, sticking the needle into his right leg in one fast, fluid motion.

"Sophie, call 911," she said. "Go! Now!" *Fast*, he thought, *she was so fast*. It made him feel calm even though his heart was racing, his limbs were jackhammering, and his vision was going blurry around the edges. She smiled at him and her face was kind. "It's okay," she said. "You're okay now."

Her eyes were very blue. They were the last thing he saw as he plummeted through the floor and into dark waters where there was no air and the lights flickered at the surface, even as the music beckoned him deeper—the same melody Sophie had sung to him earlier. His mom bent over him and mussed his hair. His baby sister was born and he took her in his arms, brave enough to take her this time; he had been afraid before. The music grew louder. He could breathe now. He was grateful.

Chapter 1
July 11, 12:00 p.m.

Isaac fervently wished he hadn't worn shorts. Besides the fact that the grass under his thighs was itchy, his legs were too skinny. It was obvious here, in a crowd of other teenagers, the way it hadn't been at home, or in the dressing room at American Eagle Outfitters when he had shopped there for new summer clothes. His mom had waited nervously outside the dressing room—prepared to smile, he was now sure, no matter what he looked like. "You look great," she had assured him. But he was thinner and softer than the other guys assigned to his cabin, who sat casually on the grass nearby, surely not thinking about their legs at all. He reminded himself to work out more, but there were no weights at camp. Lunges and squats, that would do it. He didn't need to be huge, just a little stronger. He had always been fast enough to outrun the bullies—well, almost always—and there were always trees to climb when he couldn't get away, but he wasn't very strong. Not yet.

He brought his attention back to the present, like Michelle was always telling him to do. Kids were stirring, starting to get restless. The camp director, Ty, was wrapping up his speech. It was the same as last time: the "we're all a family" talk. Inspiring stuff, but Isaac had heard it before. A trio of girls, nested together on the grass, were whispering together and glancing in his direction. He gave in to a split second of panic—were they talking about him?—but no, their gaze was trained behind him, on a handsome guy he recognized from a couple of years back: Paul something. He'd been a camper then, but judging from the clipboard in his hands and his orange Heritage Camp T-shirt, it looked like he was a counselor now.

People were getting up now, and Isaac scrambled to do the same. Handsome Paul something was walking toward him and saying his name. Isaac forced a smile and joined the group of boys clustered around Paul while the girls ran off in another direction. Kids were moving everywhere, and the noise was amazing. He had forgotten about all the shouting and screaming that happened at camp. Paul's voice was surprisingly soft, and he had to strain to hear him.

"Isaac? You're new this year, right?"

"Yes," he heard himself say. "Brand new."

"My name's Paul Anderson. You're in C Cabin, right? I'm your counselor. Do you have a buddy yet?"

Isaac cringed. He had forgotten the buddy system. "No, actually."

"Let me introduce you to someone," Paul said. "He knows everyone, and he'll get you all set up." He called out to a group of kids over by the lodge. "Hal?"

A slender brown-skinned boy in sunglasses turned and nodded. Isaac didn't think he'd ever seen him before. The boy looked back at the girl he'd been talking to for a moment, and then they parted. Isaac realized who the girl was and felt his palms get damp. He wiped them on his stupid shorts as the kid, who was wearing a T-shirt with what looked like a TARDIS on it, approached. Isaac noticed he had skinny legs too. But he strode toward them without a trace of the self-consciousness that dogged Isaac at every step. His hair was tightly curled, cut close to his scalp, and his smile was open.

"Salutations, my friend. A pleasure to see you," he said to Paul.

Paul grinned at Isaac, though his words were directed at the other boy. "You too, dude. Isaac, this is Hal Shaw. Hal, this is Isaac, he's new. Can you introduce him around?"

"Certainly," Hal said. It was hard to tell how old he might be. He was wearing wraparound shades that reminded Isaac of pictures he'd seen from the eighties—shiny and reflective. He turned to Isaac for a long moment and cocked his head. Isaac had a sense of being... scanned. "Whose acquaintance would you like to make first?"

"Um," Isaac said. "I'm not sure."

"A systematic approach, then. We shall start with the Pauls, I think. There is quite a surplus of them, if you haven't noticed," he said. He jerked his head toward the lodge and they started walking that way, across the long green field that Isaac knew would serve for endless games of Sharks and Minnows, elbow tag, and Heritage Olympics.

"No, I—"

"There really are quite a lot. I'm developing an explanatory hypothesis. I think it has to do with church. You know how Heritage Camp started?" Hal asked.

Isaac thought he probably did know but had forgotten. He shook his head.

Hal recited it briskly, like something he'd memorized. "Hank and Thelma Lee, inspired by Christian charity, adopted seven children from Korea after the war, literally arranging an Act of Congress to do so. Their church brethren found this inspiring and many followed suit; Evangelicals love Paul, hence, a superfluous number of them. I was a Paul myself, but I changed my name."

Isaac had a lot of questions, but he settled on the one that seemed safest: "Did your parents mind?"

But they were now at the timbered porch, and Hal ignored the question. Isaac felt a little rush of nerves as about a dozen kids turned toward them, smiling at Hal, who said, "Let me introduce you to everyone." Their faces were open and curious as they looked at Isaac. He saw no sign of recognition.

Later that evening, Isaac slipped his Chromebook out of the duffel bag under his bed and went looking for Ty. He found him in the lodge, sitting at the end of one of the long tables they used at meals.

"Hey there! What can I do for you, my man?" Ty asked.

"Um, I'm Isaac Whitson. My parents said I could use the office once a day? For email?"

"Isaac, of course. I remember. Do you know where it is? Here, follow me." He backed away from the table and headed toward a little room off the kitchen. It was a bit messy, with boxes on the floor and two desks strewn with papers. One of the boxes overflowed with orange T-shirts. A counselor he recognized as Katie was kneeling on the floor, removing art supplies from the other box. She glanced up at Isaac and smiled, then looked at Ty, who said, "Katie, this is my friend Isaac, and he's going to use the office for a bit. You need privacy, my man?"

"No, not really. I mean, just away from the cabin is fine." Isaac hoped he wasn't blushing. The arrangement with Michelle was embarrassing—he had to email her once a day for the first two weeks—but it was the price of coming to camp. He couldn't cope with anyone looking over his shoulder, so this was the deal.

Katie asked, "Are you sure? I can find somewhere else to be. There should be fresh cookies pretty soon too. Why don't I bring you some?"

"I'm fine, really. I just need a few minutes," Isaac said.

Katie swept a pile of T-shirts off one of the chairs and invited him to sit. "I'll just keep sorting the art supplies, then." She gave him a warm smile. Isaac smiled back, then sat down and opened his computer.

The door opened and the camp nurse came in. "Hi, Katie. Oh, hello," she said, seeing Isaac. "I forget your name, I'm sorry."

"Isaac."

The nurse smiled at him briefly and went on. "Katie, I need to have all the counselor medications too. I don't need to keep them in the office, but I have to log them in."

"Oh, okay. Did everyone not do that already?"

"No, none of the counselors did. Can you let them know? It's an ACA requirement."

"Of course," Katie said. "I'll make sure they do it by tomorrow morning, if that's okay?"

"Great. See you later, Isaac."

He nodded, then went back to his email.

July 11

Michelle,

This feels really stupid but I promised, so here goes.

Heritage Camp, Day 1.

No one even looked at me. That's the big news of the day. I saw lots of people I recognized but nobody did a double take. Nobody even said "You look familiar." After all that role-playing we did in case that happened! Maybe it's the broken nose. I should send that guy a thank-you note. Does the restraining order work both ways?

Kidding.

It's hot. And humid. Not like normal Oregon weather at all.

So, some people I know already. I remember my counselor, but he doesn't remember me. And there's Nathan, my CIT. He used to be a dorky kid picked last in sports. Still is, but he seems happy with himself. Really nice guy. You said to try one person who seems approachable, and he's the one I picked because he was so welcoming (and because it was so obvious he didn't recognize me).

Then there's my "buddy," Hal. Very…different. Obviously different is okay with me, so there's that. But even though I like him a lot, he's extremely popular and everyone at camp wants to visit and catch up with him. Nathan is a good guy, the kind my grandpa would call a good egg. But Hal is a trip. Maybe more of an Easter egg. For one thing, he wears sunglasses at all times, indoors and out. I haven't asked him why. And he's a walking dictionary. Or is it a thesaurus? I've been trying to keep track of all the new words he uses. At my old school he would have been beaten up and stuffed in a locker.

Food's not bad but lots of fried things. We're supposed to swim tomorrow.

Isaac

Chapter 2

July 12, 8:00 a.m.

In the morning, Isaac opened his eyes, looked around, and realized he was really there—really at Heritage Camp, really in C Cabin, really at the precipice of six weeks that he could spend coasting downhill, just being himself. For a moment, he felt pierced by a bolt of such pure joy he didn't know what to do. He pulled his pillow over his face to hide his smile.

Hal cleared his throat conspicuously, bringing Isaac fully awake. Hal was standing by Isaac's bunk, dressed, with his reflective wraparound sunglasses firmly in place. The cabin was otherwise empty, although Nathan was standing at the open door and peering in. "Good morning!" he called when he saw Isaac.

Hal said, "You're welcome to forgo breakfast, Isaac, but I don't recommend it. Nathan will be devastated if he misses the French toast and, taking his CIT duties rather seriously, he won't leave without us."

Isaac got out of bed, slid on his shoes, and mumbled an apology for oversleeping.

"You're already dressed? Excellent," Hal said, and they headed toward the lodge.

When they got there, Nathan steered them toward the table where C Cabin ate their meals. This meant joining the twins, Max and David, who Isaac remembered were originally from Colombia and now lived in Sacramento; a kid named Joon with long, low-riding shorts and an attitude, whom Isaac had mentally dubbed Skater Boy; and Paul. Everyone already had bacon and French toast, and there were plastic jugs of juice and milk on the table. Paul smiled at them as they arrived.

"Hey. Have a seat and grab some chow. Did you sleep well?" Isaac nodded and slid into his seat. They were finishing up with fruit salad when Ty announced that Tanya Miller, the camp's new resident therapist, was going to address them. A petite woman stood up to speak, but the campers kept chatting. To quiet everyone, she simply raised one hand in the air and waited. "That means conversation must cease," Hal explained in a low voice. Slowly, everyone in the room began to raise their own hands. When a virtual forest of hands had sprouted and it was silent, she spoke.

"Hello, Heritage Camp!" People clapped and a few started to whoop and whistle, but it was tentative. It seemed that nobody knew the therapist very well yet. She was extremely pretty, Isaac noticed, and her smile was filled with warmth. As she went on, he noticed she had a trace of an accent. "Welcome to our summer session. As you already know, I am new here. But I am really delighted to be here and excited to work with you.

"We are all unique individuals. I've looked over your paperwork, and you are an amazing group of people. We have cheerleaders and writers and musicians here. We have athletes and even a national judo champion!" Suddenly everyone was looking toward the C Cabin boys. Isaac stopped chewing, feeling nervous.

"Hal Shaw!" someone whooped, and everyone went nuts. Hal raised his spoon to the crowd and continued eating, but he looked pleased. A boy from the next table reached over to thump him on the back.

Isaac turned to Nathan. "No way."

"Way," he confirmed. Isaac's eyes widened. "I know, right? He's also some kind of superhacker. I don't even understand half of what he does."

Tanya continued. "We have campers from as far away as Florida and as close as Portland. Cheer when you hear your country, if you want. We have campers here who were born in China!" Cheers. "The Philippines!" A few claps. "Haiti!" One girl whooped as loud as she could and everyone laughed. "Ethiopia!" Somehow the silence that followed this converged on a single girl who sat perfectly still, looking frightened. Tanya Miller moved on quickly. "Cambodia! Colombia! Vietnam! Thailand!" Loud whoops and lots of clapping.

"But all of us have one big thing in common: we are all adoptees. Yes, that includes me. I came to the US from Thailand when I was much younger. And part of my process has been to integrate all the aspects of myself into one identity. Integration means putting together into a coherent whole. I am American. I am Thai. I am a therapist. I am also a graduate student, a vegetarian, and a candy addict!" She smiled and some of the kids laughed a little. "All these things are equally me. Just like all of you have many aspects that make up who you are.

"Sometimes for adoptees, these things can go to war with one another inside of us. We ask ourselves things like, 'Am I Asian or am I white? If my whole family is white, and I am African—am I still part of my family? Is my mom really my mom? Am I this or am I that?' And there are no easy answers, except that maybe we can be more than one thing. You might not fit neatly in a box. Our experience can be richer for it. And what I'll be doing this summer with you wonderful campers is helping you work through these interesting and important questions. Make sense? Does anyone have a question for me right now?"

Am I this or am I that? Isaac thought it made plenty of sense.

Joon called out, "So, like, what exactly will we be doing?" There were chuckles from around the room.

"Some writing," Tanya said. "Some talking. Some art. Our work together will be age-appropriate, so you ten-year-olds will be doing something different from the thirteens, who will be doing something different from the sixteens. And what you share in the workshops is confidential, which we will go over in more depth when we're in smaller groups. I may share some of my general findings with the people I work with, because I'm also a researcher. But your name will never be attached to anything. And if you don't want me to use something that you say or do in a workshop, I will respect that completely.

"Also, anyone who wants to meet with me privately is welcome to do so. I have regular hours that are posted on my cabin door, and I'm also available during your evening free time. Just stop by. I'll even share my candy."

July 12

Michelle,

I haven't had a session with the therapist but don't worry, I met her today. She's busy like ALL the time. Her name is Tanya Miller and incidentally, she's also from Thailand. I feel fine. I'll see her most days anyway because she runs all the workshops in case someone needs counseling after we discuss things like racial identity and birth mothers and abandonment issues. I met the camp nurse, even though I'm not taking the pills anymore (I thought it would be embarrassing to get them from her, which is partly why I switched to shots) but she seems nice, it probably would have been nbd.

Her daughter is a camper. I could be in trouble there. I remember her from before. She was my crush then and is possibly even prettier than before. I think I won't mention her name, she can be X.

Isaac

July 13

Michelle,

Swimming was okay. Lots of kids wear swim shirts, it turns out, because their parents don't want them to get sunburned. Nathan says most of the parents are overprotective. His actually stayed in a motel down the street the first time he came to camp, just in case he needed them. And X's mother comes to camp every year to keep an eye on her, he says (although she is the camp nurse, and X has diabetes and needs injections, so personally I think that's understandable).

I think that X is dating my counselor, Paul. It figures. He's older, better looking, and unfortunately, too nice to hate.

Isaac

July 14

Michelle,

Today our workshop was called "speed-dating" and involved talking to lots of different people for three minutes at a time. We were supposed to share something about ourselves that most people wouldn't be able to tell by looking. (I came up with "I'm homeschooled," which fit the bill nicely.)

I learned that Paul has social anxiety (yes, the counselors also participate in workshops), that a girl named Piper's grandma died two days before camp started and she feels guilty for being here, that there are at least three other Pauls (long story), and that X is hilarious as well as beautiful. I'll try to reproduce our conversation, which is the first time we've really talked face-to-face. Picture my palms sweating for verisimilitude (that's a Hal word).

X - What's my secret? Go ahead, guess.

Me - You're Sophie, right?

X - Wrong. That's my name but not my secret. Never mind, I'll guess yours. You're actually a girl.

Me - (speechless)

X - Just kidding. Let me see…you're not an adoptee at all. You're a spy from China like the trolls say.

Me - (stupidly) I'm not from China.

Bell rings, end of conversation. And now I realize that the stupidity has spilled into this email, where I have now revealed Sophie's name…

Isaac

Chapter 3

July 15, 8:00 a.m.

On the way to breakfast, Nathan told Isaac, "We'll start the film contest today. Do you know what that's about?"

That must be new, Isaac thought. "Uh-uh."

"Well, you'll soon find out! Let's go in."

The rules of the seventy-two-hour short-film competition were simple. Teams had three days to put together a five-to-six-minute piece; the theme was "fitting in." They had to use a canoe oar as a prop somewhere, and they had to include the line "It's not what it looks like."

It's not what it looks like. Isaac tried not to read too much into this line.

Including Hal and Isaac, there were five people on the team: a nine-year-old girl called Eliza; Sophie, who insisted on joining the same group as Hal; and Nathan, who explained that he preferred to be behind the camera.

"Can I be a pirate, please, Hal? I want to be a pirate," Sophie said, stomping around the picnic table where they sat in the shade. "That white whale took me leg! Arr!"

Hal smiled and shook his head ever so slightly.

Eliza asked, "Can we have fairy pirates? I want to be a fairy pirate."

"Great idea, sweetie," Sophie said. She sat back down. "Well? What do you guys think?"

"Or a mermaid," the little girl said. "The kind with wings."

"I am open to suggestions, of course," said Hal. "I did have some ideas, none of which, regrettably, have heretofore included pirates or mermaids."

"Wings *and* a tail," Eliza added.

"What ideas?" Isaac asked. Everyone was looking to Hal, clearly the group leader. Isaac had noticed it was always like this. Hal had a weird manner of expressing himself, but he was confident in a way that few people managed to be. Not conspicuously, though; he was just very much himself. And, Isaac realized, Hal was never unkind. Not that he went around doing good deeds or anything; it was just that he didn't even bother with the ordinary ways in which teenage boys tested their strength on each other or put each other down. Isaac had borne the brunt of unkindness too many times not to be touched by that fact.

"I had in mind a whodunit: a mystery. No murders allowed, unfortunately. The counselors feel that homicidal violence might frighten the younger kids—present company excluded, of course." He nodded at Eliza.

"Um, that's okay," the little girl said.

"So"—Hal clapped his hands—"the theft of a valuable item. Someone will need to hide said item in a place that's difficult to access. Another character will obtain clues and retrieve the object."

"The fairy pirate!" cried Eliza. "She can get into anywhere, I bet."

"Indeed, you are gifted with fairy-like proportions," said Hal. She frowned at him.

"You can fit in a small place," Sophie explained.

"Fitting in!" Nathan said. "That takes care of our theme."

"So what's the booty and how do we lift it?" Sophie asked.

"I'm not sure," Hal said. "Something small and light enough to carry, but not so small that we can't see it easily. It should fit in a canoe."

"The camp flag?" Nathan suggested.

"That's been done for real so many times, it's not even funny. How about a couple of rolls of toilet paper?" Sophie said. "TP is always going missing here, and the counselors are constantly hollering about it." Nobody commented on that idea.

"How about the clarinet?" Isaac asked. "The one Paul plays at AGT?"

"Now that is a highly viable idea," Hal said thoughtfully.

"Everyone will recognize it. And it's small enough to hide," Isaac said. "But will he let us use it?"

"It's probably pretty valuable," Nathan said.

"I can talk him into it," Sophie said. Hal raised an eyebrow at her, questioning. Then she added, "I have my ways."

They spent the rest of the session discussing how the theft might work, who would swipe the item (Captain Jackie Chickadee), and who would retrieve the booty (the mermaid-fairy-pirate, naturally) to great hoopla.

"Isaac, of course, will apprehend the thief in the final act," Hal said.

"Wait, what?" Isaac stammered. He didn't like that idea at all. He'd even asked his parents not to sign the media-release form that would let Heritage Camp use his picture in its promotional materials. "Why me?"

"You're the obvious hero. Not me."

"You get to apprehend me," Sophie said and grinned wickedly. "And I won't go down without a fight. I might kick. I might even bite."

"See, there you have it," Isaac said lightly. "This calls for a national judo champion."

"Ooh!" said Sophie. "I've always wanted to be put in a head-lock." But there was something a bit false in her tone. He'd noticed it before—how she made these provocative jokes, even though it didn't seem like she found them very funny.

"Isaac will figure it out, but he'll get a few details wrong," Hal said. "Then we'll explain it all in the denouement."

"We only have five minutes," Nathan said, raising an index finger. "We can't afford a denouement."

"We can omit the denouement. But I don't want to do any acting. I'm sorry, Isaac, but it's either got to be you or Nathan."

"Me? Why me?" said Nathan, sounding panicked. "I'm the cinematographer! I don't want to be in movies!"

"What is wrong with you guys?" Sophie asked. "This is a film contest. Did you not hear the part where some of you will have to be filmed?"

"I don't mind," Eliza piped up. "I can be a fairy pirate *and* a fairy detective."

"Oh, for fuck's sake," said Sophie.

"Sophie! Language!" Nathan said.

"Sorry." She bounced her forehead lightly off the table several times. Just then Isaac saw Ty coming down the path, heading in their general direction.

"Hey, I have an idea," Isaac said. "What if we ask Ty? It could be like a cameo."

"The detective isn't a cameo, is it?" asked Nathan.

"Why Ty?" asked Sophie.

"Because he happens to be coming over here," Isaac said. "And everyone knows him."

"Ty is a rather obvious choice," Hal said. "And Nathan is correct: the detective is hardly a small role. But what if we make him the thief? Or the mastermind behind the thief, with Eliza doing the actual thievery? Then Sophie could play the detective—the pirate detective, of course. Ty? Could we bother you for a moment?"

"How's it going, peeps?" Ty smiled at them. "Isaac, my man! Hal, Nathan, Sophie. My new friend Eliza. Everything awesome here?"

"Fairly awesome," Hal said.

"We need a bad guy," Eliza said. "Are you a good bad guy?"

"I'm afraid I have to be the bad guy right now, friends," said Ty, "because Tanya is expecting everyone at an important meeting. So for now, that's a wrap. Lodge in five...or else." He gave an exaggerated sneer and narrowed his eyes at Eliza until she giggled.

"See?" Isaac said. "He's going to be a great villain."

July 16

Michelle,

So, there was a big meeting yesterday and I wonder, have you heard of the Hague Convention on adoption? Tanya (therapist) works for them and she's doing some sort of research. I had to sign a waiver. Well, I didn't HAVE to sign, but I did because she's only using some of the stuff we write in our workshops, which are anonymous, so it seemed like an okay idea. Plus, everyone else signed and if I didn't, it would have attracted more attention than just signing. Do you think this was okay? Or should I go to her and cancel my signature? She said we can do that if we change our minds.

Isaac

July 17

Michelle,

Nothing else interesting to report. I emailed my mom but maybe you could let her know I'm fine too. I can tell from her emails that she doesn't believe me, or at least she still worries.

Isaac

P.S. Still fine. Really.

July 18

Michelle,

Remember when I said Hal would have been stuffed in a locker at Woodrow Wilson High? I forgot to tell you I was wrong. Turns out he's a national judo champion. Correction: he's THE national judo champion in his age group. I might not have believed it except for what happened today. The twins in our cabin were picking on Nathan a bit and Hal asked them politely to stop. (Actually, what he said was "This conversation must cease immediately.") Max said something like "Or what? You going to go all Jackie Chan on my ass?" while his brother, David, sort of chuckled and puffed up his chest. Hal said that Jackie

Chan actually does kung fu, not judo, and the twins said something like "Same thing," to which Hal said, "Not remotely the same thing." Then Max did that horrible thing that people do with their eyes when they're making fun of Asian people, David started laughing hysterically, and Nathan (who's from Korea) said they were both being stupid and immature, but I could tell he was about to cry. And then they picked on Nathan some more, and then Hal moved so fast I didn't see anything, and then they were both on the floor screaming "Uncle!" while he held their arms behind their backs. With ONE FINGER. I mean two fingers total, but one on each arm. "Apologize," he said. "And I shall also require you to grovel." Which they did.

As I write this I am hearing you in my mind asking, "What were you feeling?" and "What did you do next?" Well, Michelle, I did a whole lot of jack squat. And what I was feeling? I don't even know. Although it was fun to see the twins mashed into the floor and, later, picking the grit out of their faces.

As you know, I'm a coward...only now Hal knows it too, and so does Nathan.

Isaac

July 19

Michelle,

Do you think I'm the only person at camp writing to their therapist? I think I must be, but if you ask me, there are plenty of people here who need it more than I do. There are girls crying all the time, lots of drama. It's sort of like high school with almost no white people, and no one seems to want to beat the shit out of me.

I tried to visit with Tanya one-on-one, as you keep asking me to do. This time I got as far as her cabin before turning around and climbing a tree. (Noble fir, if you're wondering.)

It's not that I chickened out. There were voices coming from the cabin...yelling voices. I heard "research" and "unacceptable" and something like "hippo" or "hippa"? I don't know. And a few seconds after I got settled on my branch, the door banged open and out came the camp nurse, who was red in the face and practically steaming. Tanya came out and watched her storm away, then went in and closed the door.

Seriously, do you expect me to walk into that?

Anyway, still fine.

We're making a movie for camp. More on that later. I have to go eat my daily allotment of tater tots and sheet cake.

Isaac

July 20

Michelle,

I'm not trying to be funny but I cannot figure out girls. You and I have talked in the past about nonverbal cues, how to read people, stuff like that. What about a girl who acts super tough but other times seems…like, breakable? Fragile, like one of those little glass animals my grandmother collects? Who tells dirty jokes but has an invisible force field around her body? I'm talking about Sophie, of course.

She's beautiful and seems unhappy. (Hey, we have one thing in common.) She has at least one good friend, though. Hal. They seem to be pretty close. She broke the rules and came to our cabin today, supposedly to look for Paul, but I think she really wanted to talk to Hal. For half a second I thought she might be there for me, but no.

Piper likes me, apparently. And I like Sophie, and Sophie seems to like Paul, and I can't tell who Paul likes, although he spends a surprising amount of time with Tanya (the aforementioned therapist and no, I haven't consulted her privately because again, I'M FINE), and Hal is very possibly a robot. Seriously. Maybe that's why he wears those silly shades all the time. He's always on his laptop, and when I ask what he's up to he says, "Genotypes and phenotypes." I had to google those words and I still have no idea what he's doing (maybe you do?). Nathan says Hal came in third in the Intel science fair last year and is going for gold this year.

What am I doing? How do I feel about it? I'm watching, and listening, and thinking. As for how I feel, reference above: FINE. A bit crushy.

Isaac

P.S. Seriously, what are genotypes and phenotypes?

July 23

Michelle,

Still fine. We did have some excitement today. There was a fire in one of the cabins, not mine. A fire engine came and everything. My counselor went running over to put it out, as he's the hero type (who always gets the girl lol). Camp director came looking for me afterwards. He asked me to keep an eye out for inappropriate substances in my cabin. If Axe body spray counts as a fire hazard, then I ought to point him at the twins, but I'm not going to squeal on anyone. I have a feeling he's referring to my counselor, though.

Isaac

Chapter 4
July 24, 3:30 p.m.

Isaac found himself alone in the cabin for a change after a nature hike ended early. The excursion leader felt sick and sent everyone back without regard for the buddy system as she stumbled off to the infirmary, trying not to puke. So Isaac pulled out his Chromebook in the cabin.

July 24

Michelle,

It's been nice writing to you, but I think I can take it from here since our two weeks is up. Thanks for everything. See you in September.

Isaac

After he hit send, he felt lighter. He'd made it through the first two weeks of camp. He had friends. He liked a girl, and while she didn't appear to reciprocate his feelings, she didn't seem to hate him, either.

And he felt...like himself. It was nice; a warm feeling. In the glow of that warmth, he decided to email his parents, something he'd been meaning to do.

July 24

Mom and Dad,

It's a lot of fun here. I don't think you needed to worry at all. We spend a lot of time talking about adoption, and it's made me a little curious about some of the details. I might ask you some questions when I get home. Not a big deal. The food is great, although Mom, you might not approve of all the fried stuff. I'm making friends. Yes, friends! Both guys and girls. We do a lot of sports, although I am not any better now than ever. I am getting slightly more fit, I think. Also, I am very tanned. You might not know me lol. Overall, seriously, you can relax. This was a great idea, thank you for sending me.

Love, Isaac

Someone's phone made a sound—a pleasant, musical noise, like water dropping onto a tin roof. Isaac ignored it until it happened again. *Ba-loop.* The sound was coming from Paul's bunk. Isaac didn't want to spy. But was it really spying? It might be an urgent message. *If it looks that way,* Isaac thought, *I'll go find him.* As if to underscore the urgency, it ba-looped again.

Isaac picked it up and swiped the screen to open it, and for a moment, he couldn't take in what he was seeing. It was a wobbly, slightly blurry video—a girl bending over a table, crushing up a pill, then leaning over to sniff the powder into her nose. And then she fell back, smiling. As she fell, her shirt pulled away from her abdomen so that there was a flash of bare skin. It replayed again and again. By the third time, Isaac understood that he was looking at Sophie.

He shoved the phone away like it was a living thing, some dangerous animal, his heart going a million miles an hour. The horror of it. And that flash of skin—there was a sensation of heat, almost pain, in a part of his body that he generally ignored. He closed his eyes and helplessly saw the image again, imprinted behind his eyelids. *Oh, Sophie*, he thought, *what are you doing to yourself?*

Should he tell someone? If so, who? She would hate him, wouldn't she?

Isaac left the cabin and walked fast through the woods to the water's edge. He could hear some of the younger kids playing, so he walked in the opposite direction. Indecisive, he headed toward Tanya Miller's cabin. Without thinking about it, without thinking about anything, he climbed a tree. He chose a difficult one, a pine without branches close to the ground, so he had to throw his arms and legs around the tree and shimmy upward, scraping the insides of his thighs. He almost relished the pain. He reached a branch, pulled himself up, and sat.

He could see Tanya's cabin from there. He reached up to the next branch and climbed a little higher. This was an old behavior and Michelle would not approve—climbing high enough to hide, high enough to get really hurt if he should fall. Tanya was moving about inside. As he watched, Paul came out the door and headed down the path toward C Cabin. Isaac stayed very still, but Paul, appearing tense, didn't even look up.

By craning his head in the opposite direction from Tanya's place, Isaac could just see the infirmary through the branches. There was movement behind the windows. He calmed himself by thinking of the nurse inside, possibly soothing her patient, the counselor with the stomach bug. It would be nice—lying on cool sheets, sipping apple juice. If Isaac fell from here, he'd probably break an arm, at least. Then he would be sent home.

His own room; his refuge. A safe place. And a lonely one.

Isaac was not so lost in thought that he didn't see Tanya walking up to the tree, but it startled him when she spoke.

"That's pretty high," she called. "You must have some real skill."

"Well, you know. Years of practice." His voice was high and unsteady.

"I hope you won't fall," she said. "Can I tempt you down with a cup of tea?"

"I'm not sure that will help."

"Having a hard day?" she asked. "I am too. Come on down. Maybe you can cheer me up."

"Give me a minute," Isaac said. He stared at the branches above and took ten deep, calming breaths, as Michelle had taught him. He counted each breath, concentrating on the cool air coming into his nose and the warm air going out again. By the end of the second breath, he was no longer tempted to let go of the trunk. By the tenth breath he was actually afraid he might fall by accident, and he knew it was time to climb down. Isaac landed without incident on the pine-needle floor.

He and Tanya walked, without talking, to her cabin.

"I've actually been meaning to come to you," Isaac admitted. "I was supposed to. But I've been doing fine, so I didn't bother."

She didn't say anything right away. Instead, she made tea, plugging in an electric kettle and getting out cups, spoons, and a selection of boxes filled with tea bags.

"It still smells like smoke in here," she said. "Would you rather sit outside?"

"Oh, right," he said. "Yesterday. The fire. That must have been... was it scary?"

She shook her head. "I was not here when it started," she said. "It only required a fire extinguisher. Tea?"

Isaac picked Constant Comment. "My mom is addicted to this stuff," he said. The sharp, orangey smell reminded him of home.

"Mm. I like it too," she said. "But no caffeine for me this late in the day. I'd be up all night."

In silence, they watched the tea steep. Isaac thought about telling her what he'd seen. Would Sophie hate him? He was considering the question when Tanya spoke.

"Can I ask? Why were you 'supposed' to see me?"

"I have a therapist at home—Michelle. She thought I should probably check in at camp. But I've been doing just, like, perfectly fine."

"Okay. What led you to start therapy?"

"Well, I was bullied kind of big-time at my old school. I'm home-schooled now."

"I'm so sorry to hear you were bullied. Can I ask what happened?"

"Someone broke my nose in a couple of places, for one thing," Isaac said, smiling to show he was over it. Because he was, really.

"Oh, that's terrible. Serious bullying, then."

"I guess so. But that was a year ago."

"Has anyone at camp made you feel uncomfortable? Or unsafe?"

"No, not at all. I really like it here," Isaac reassured her.

"How did the altercation happen? The punch in the nose?"

Stalling, Isaac looked around a bit. Her office was pretty spare. There was a sink and cabinet. Just a couple of chairs, a spider plant. There was a trifold screen dividing the room, probably hiding the door to her bedroom. Or maybe her bed was in the same room. He thought of Paul coming and going, the way he'd bolted to her cabin when they noticed the smoke...of her bed, behind the screen.

He felt a dawning, awful comprehension, and he knew he couldn't tell her about Sophie.

"Someone had the wrong idea about me," Isaac said. Her face bore an expression of professional compassion, and suddenly he felt angry. "They thought I was a pushover."

"Isaac. Isaac!"

Isaac opened his eyes. As usual, he experienced a tiny thrill at awaking in the cabin. It was dark, everyone was asleep, and someone was whispering outside the window. It was Piper, the girl who had cried during the speed-dating workshop. She wasn't crying now; instead, she was grinning and wiggling her fingers at him.

"Come to the party," she whispered. "Shh. Just you."

He checked his phone: it was 2:00 a.m. He got up as quietly as he could, slid into flip-flops, and pulled on a hoodie. He hoped he looked okay, but it was dark and besides, it was the first time he could recall being invited to a party in a couple of years. He ran his hands through his hair and hoped for the best. He glanced at Paul, who looked asleep but tense, clutching his pillow like a life preserver. Hal slept flat on his back, his hands curled on top of his chest. Without sunglasses, his face looked vulnerable. His naked eyelids, so rarely seen, fluttered a bit.

Piper was alone outside. She shushed Isaac silently and gestured for him to follow her. They were headed to the beach path. As they got closer to the water, Isaac heard quiet voices and smelled cigarette smoke. Several people were sitting on logs or on the pine-needle floor. "This is Isaac," Piper announced. Sophie, three other girls, and one apparent couple looked up with mild interest. The guy—*one of the Pauls*, Isaac thought—nodded at him and said "'Sup." One girl quietly plucked a ukulele.

"Welcome to the nicotine-and-wine insomnia club," Sophie said. She tossed Isaac a tiny plastic bottle that sloshed with red liquid. "Single-serving Oregon pinot noir. My mom hoards these. Help yourself. Lower the old inhibitions."

Isaac didn't think he needed his inhibitions lowered. Not yet, anyway.

"No thanks," he said.

"Smoke, then?" she asked.

"Okay."

She lit a cigarette in her mouth and handed it over. The filter end was slightly damp from her lips. Isaac inhaled and his chest instantly seized up, on fire; he coughed slightly, trying to expel the smoke without making a scene. Unfortunately, there was a reserve of smoke left in his mouth, which he involuntarily inhaled deep into his lungs, sending himself into a paroxysm of coughing that made everyone laugh.

"Dude," said the boy. "Don't cough up a lung."

"Noob!" giggled Piper. "Try again."

"I don't think so," Isaac said and tried to smile, handing the cigarette back to Sophie, who took it.

"Are you in training?" Sophie asked.

Isaac goggled. Did he look like an athlete?

"Not exactly," he said.

"Well? How come you're no fun? I thought you might be fun. All the boys around here are so lame," Piper complained.

"Not all of them," another girl teased.

"Shut up! Slut."

"Leave him alone. Isaac bunks with Hal," said Sophie. "I should have thought of that. Hal will totally notice if you smoke." She opened the wine and drained it. "Put the empties in my bag," she instructed the group. "I'm going for a walk." She looked a little unsteady as she picked her way across the boulders and logs, her right leg appearing to hesitate, just a little, as she made her way toward the boathouse.

"Shouldn't someone go after her?" Isaac asked.

"Not me," said Piper. "I need my head, thanks."

"Go right ahead," said the boy. As Isaac walked away, he heard him mutter, "Just don't get your hopes up."

Sophie was sitting on the dock. "Bye-bye," she said as Isaac walked up. "Nice knowing you." But she wasn't talking to Isaac. She was waving at her flip-flop, which was drifting away on the surface of the lake. He hoped she wouldn't swim out for it, since she seemed a little tipsy; he waded out to grab it until the water reached his knees, but it was too far gone. He took an oar from the boathouse and managed to retrieve the sandal.

"My glass slipper," she said as Isaac handed it over. "Thank you, kind sir."

"You're welcome."

"No. No, that's not your line. You say, 'Oh, it was you I danced with last night. I've been searching the land.'"

"Oh, right," Isaac said, trying to smile. "I recognize you now. Weren't you wearing something a little different?"

"Why, yes," she said. "Allow me to change. Close your eyes. Close them!"

He did. After a few seconds he heard a slight *thunk*, then a splash. He felt his own sandal sliding off his right foot. When he opened his eyes, Sophie was in the water, holding his flip-flop in one hand. A pile of clothing sat beside him. And her prosthetic leg, something he had only ever seen attached to her body, had made the *thunk*. It looked odd and inert, lying there.

Isaac pretended he didn't see her in the water and just stared at her clothes. His heart was pounding, but he kept his tone light. "Oh my God," he said, "Sophie's been raptured."

"No," she said, "I'm a mermaid. See?"

She waggled her one foot in the water like a fin, as if she were a little kid. "Maybe you should come on out," Isaac said. "Get dressed? It's cold." For a second he thought he'd have to go in after her. But she hauled herself onto the dock with her elbows. He averted his eyes, but in his peripheral vision he still saw her white body in the moonlight, her leg that ended just below the knee. She pulled on her clothes and sat beside him, dripping. They were close enough that the water from her hair landed on his arm, every drop making him shiver—and not from being chilly. She pulled another tiny wine bottle out of her pocket, opened it, and took a lengthy drink. "Cold," she said.

"Take my hoodie."

"Thanks." She let him drape it over her, watching his face. "Does this gross you out?" she asked, gesturing at her prosthesis on the dock.

"No."

"Good. I believe you."

"Good," Isaac said.

"You don't seem like a liar. Unlike some people."

"Glad to hear that," he said, trying to sound casual. He felt guilty.

"Have you ever done something you shouldn't have?" she asked. "Because you seem like the most careful guy I've ever met."

"Careful? What does that mean?"

"I don't know. You just...it's hard to picture you losing control. Losing your temper, doing something stupid."

"I've done plenty of stupid things," he protested.

"Name one."

"Well," he said, "I did binge-watch the first season of *American Horror Story* in a single day once, right before Halloween."

"That's nothing," she said. "What about something...something you can't come back from?"

Isaac had no idea what to say to that.

She leaned back slightly, as if to bring him into focus. Her eyes were brown today, their natural color. Without the colored lenses, her face looked almost unbearably open, almost naked, but he still found it hard to interpret her expression. She turned back to the lake and said, "Sometimes I think my whole life is just me doing one stupid thing after another."

What could he say? He had seen the video—had seen her snorting drugs, falling back in a blissed-out heap—but she couldn't know he'd seen it.

"Is there anything," he asked, "that I could maybe help you with?"

"Let's see." Her words were very slightly slurred: *let's shee*. "I'm in love with someone who wants to do something completely crazy that I can't talk him out of. I caused something really horrible to happen to someone else I loved. And now there's this...thing with me on the internet that shouldn't be, which is totally, totally my own fault. No, I don't see how you could maybe help." She stood up. "Just—don't judge me, all right?"

"Too late," Isaac said. He took a deep breath. "I've already judged you. I think you're funny and smart." *And beautiful.* "And hard on yourself. And maybe too easy on...other people."

"What would you know about that?"

"Well, if there is something out there, and you didn't put it there...if someone is holding it over your head..." *Blame Paul*, he urged silently. But she didn't say anything. "Get out from under him."

"Have you seen it?" she demanded. "That video?"

"I—" Isaac couldn't open his mouth to lie. He closed it again. "I didn't mean to," he finally said. "It just sort of appeared."

"Isaac. Where. Did it just. Appear?"

"On a phone," he replied. "I picked it up to see if it was an important message."

"Whose phone?" He shook his head. "*Whose phone?*"

He couldn't say his name. "My counselor's."

At that she pulled on her leg, stood up unsteadily, and nearly fell. Isaac tried to help her, but she said "Don't!" and walked back up to camp. He thought of going after her, but shame kept him pinioned to the dock until the sky began to lighten.

When he finally got up, all his joints stiff, and returned to the cabin, he badly needed to go to the bathroom. The guys were sleeping, but they were starting to toss around in their bunks, and Isaac knew they'd be up soon. His stomach was cramping; it was probably stress. Or maybe that stomach bug.

But it was worse. Much worse. This hadn't happened in months; it wasn't supposed to happen. He thought for a moment, trying not to panic. There were things he needed. He didn't have anything.

It was quiet at the infirmary too. He didn't want to wake anyone up, but he didn't see an alternative, as the infirmary was locked and the nurse's room was attached. When Genevieve poked her head through the door, she looked sleepy but not annoyed.

"Sorry! I slept a little late. What's up?"

"I have a stomachache. Can I just kind of hang out here for a while?"

"Sure," she said. She withdrew for a moment and came back with a key. She wore a rather long and voluminous belted bathrobe, which she held closed at the top. "Why don't you just lie down for a bit? I won't go anywhere. I'll just be on this side getting ready if you need something. Bathroom's on the left. Let me make sure it's open." She checked the door, which opened. "Sometimes I lock it from the inside and forget to unlock it. Oh, one more thing." She ducked into her own room and then back into the bathroom. "Okay, all yours. I can have some breakfast sent up later if you're up for it. Or maybe not," she added, seeing his expression. "There's water in that jug and some cups. See you soon."

Isaac stayed for the morning. While the nurse was busy giving meds, he slunk into the bathroom and locked both doors. It seemed to be the only bathroom in the building, serving the infirmary and the nurse's cabin, and there were towels and a toothbrush presumably belonging to Genevieve. Quietly he looked around, found what he needed, and did the necessaries. Then he went back and lay down in the bed. He listened to the nurse talking with the kids as she gave meds, took care of a couple of twisted ankles, treated a bee sting, and gave ibuprofen to two girls with headaches. He asked for some ibuprofen as well.

After lunch came and went, he was surprised to get visitors: Hal and Nathan.

"You were out all night and now you're sick," Nathan said sternly. "Please tell me you weren't doing something stupid."

"Oh. No, not at all. I think I just have that bug."

"Recuperate," Hal advised. "We missed you at lunch."

"You missed pizza!" Nathan said.

"But fear not. Nathan and I spent the morning editing the film, and it's nearly finished."

"I'll bring it by later," Nathan promised. "And don't forget about the dance tonight. It's after the campfire. Anything else you need, bud?"

Bud. Isaac was touched. "I'm good," he said.

But in the late afternoon, fatigue won out and Isaac took a nap that lasted until it was dark. When he woke up, everything had changed.

Chapter 5

July 25, 11:25 p.m.

Someone was howling. No—sirens.

Isaac was in the infirmary, and the lights were off. He tasted the sourness of ibuprofen on an empty stomach and hoped he wouldn't throw up. And he still ached, low in his belly.

He felt confused. Was there another fire?

Outside, red lights flashed rhythmically, throwing smears of red across the walls. He sat up and pulled back the calico curtain. The lights came from an ambulance parked in front of the lodge, right on the games field where they normally played Capture the Flag and Everybody's It. A jolt of fear displaced the nausea, and Isaac swallowed convulsively. A woman in uniform slammed the back doors of the vehicle and hustled into the driver's seat. The ambulance rolled awkwardly across the grassy field and onto the gravel drive, picked up speed, and started wailing again.

Isaac watched as the campers dispersed, kids pouring from the huge front doors of the lodge. They looked panicky and aimless, like his grandpa's chickens when the collie tried to herd them. Although the ambulance was gone, flashing lights continued to cast a weird pall on their faces—blue and green and pink, emanating from the lodge. Then suddenly, the lights stopped: the dance must be over. He could see and hear some of the older girls sobbing.

There was Sophie. She looked like she was about to collapse, propped up by friends on every side. Then she did collapse, in slow motion, her friends helping her down and shielding her from view. Her mother hurried out of the lodge, running up to the group. But she must have been repelled, as she slowly—reluctantly, it looked like—backed off.

Katie was waving her arms as though to rally the campers, but they ignored her. Ty rolled slowly down the ramp in his chair, raised his hands, and said something. He must have been more effective than his assistant, because people began to separate into groups and move toward Isaac; the infirmary lay between the lodge and the cabins. The sobs and voices grew louder as campers passed by. Isaac heard the words "couldn't breathe" and other snippets.

"Oh my God—"

"Allergic reaction—"

"Fucking kidding me—"

What the hell had happened? He should go out there, he thought. He should find Hal. He should go to Sophie.

Instead, he pulled the covers up and shivered.

When Genevieve came back to the infirmary, there was a police officer with her. The nurse must have forgotten Isaac was there. His bed was surrounded by a privacy curtain, and when the curtain stirred in the draft, he could just see the two women sitting at Genevieve's desk. The policewoman wore regular clothes, a loose auburn ponytail, and trendy black secretary glasses—but she had a gun and a badge at her hip. A tattoo emerged from her blouse and snaked up the back of her neck, but he couldn't see what it was. He stayed very still, not sure if he was supposed to be hearing their conversation, but not willing to miss it.

"I'm sorry to tell you this. As you may have expected, Paul Anderson didn't make it," the officer was saying. Her voice was very calm. Isaac felt as though his heart might stop, but instead it started pounding faster, sending the blood whooshing up into his brain. He could actually hear it behind the words the policewoman was saying: the paramedics did everything they could, *whoosh*, no one was blaming the nurse, no one was blaming anyone, *whoosh*, it was important to gather information about how this had happened, *whoosh*, *whoosh*. He closed his eyes, feeling sick.

"But the police," Genevieve was saying. "Why?"

"It's routine when there's an unexplained death, especially when it's a young person," the officer said.

"Unexplained? But do you mean that it wasn't—I mean, you do know what happened? He had an allergy. Peanuts."

"I understand."

"But we didn't allow any at camp. No peanut butter, granola bars, nothing. There are several kids with the same allergy, but Paul's is the most serious. Was. Oh God, I need to find my daughter. She'll be devastated." Genevieve's voice shook.

"This won't take long. Just tell me exactly what happened as best you can."

"I can't stop seeing his face," she whispered. "He was trying so hard to breathe. I gave him an EpiPen, but it didn't seem to do anything."

"You've given one before?"

"Many times. I work in a pediatric emergency room during the year. I know what I'm doing." Genevieve sounded defensive.

"Has it happened before, at camp?"

"Yes—not with Paul, but another camper last year, someone else with a peanut allergy. It worked immediately. I've kept one on me ever since. But he had his own too. He had already used it."

"Could they have been expired?" the cop asked. "Or gone bad?"

Genevieve shook her head. "I logged them in just a few weeks ago, checked expiration dates and inspected them. All of them, including Paul's."

"I'll need to take them anyway," the cop said.

"I don't remember what I did with them." She patted her pockets, then Isaac heard her get up and walk to the counter. Something rattled in a plastic bucket.

"They're not in the sharps container. I must have left them in the lodge. Or maybe someone picked them up."

"We'll find them," the cop said. "Did Paul take any medication?"

"He's—was—over eighteen, so he kept his own meds. But it should be on his form." The drawer slid out with a metallic click, and Isaac heard the sound of papers being shuffled. "He had an inhaler to use as needed, and allergy medicine, cetirizine. Paxil, ten milligrams at bedtime. That's an antidepressant." Isaac was surprised to hear that. Paul was a regular guy, good looking, and he had Sophie. He didn't seem like the kind of person who should need antidepressants. But you never knew.

"Was he depressed?" the cop asked.

"It says he took it for anxiety. Social anxiety."

"Did he seem depressed? Or anxious?"

"He seemed...perfect."

Isaac couldn't see her face, but in the pause that followed, he could tell the officer found this a strange response.

"Perfect?"

"Perfectly happy, content, whatever. Not depressed. What does that have to do with it? This was terrible, but why...I mean it's obviously an accident, isn't it? You can't think he did it on purpose?"

The other woman said, "Maybe you could just run me through the day. What did the campers do? What did you do?"

Genevieve took a shuddering breath. "Okay...well, breakfast is at eight. There are morning meds before and after. I usually eat later because some of the kids need to take their meds with food." She went on to describe the camp routine.

"And in the evening?"

"Dinner, a talent show. Some kids have night meds. They had a dance tonight so I was up at the lodge to make sure they got them—oh God, they're still up there! I need to get those meds. I know some of the kids missed their doses. For a lot of them it doesn't matter, but there are a few who can have seizures if they miss a pill."

"I'll walk up there with you. And here's my card. If you think of anything else, please give me a call."

The lights went off abruptly and the door banged shut—a startling sound in the quiet, even though it always banged like that—its hinges were screwy. Isaac lay back and listened to the blood pounding its way past his ears. He thought about Sophie's fury when she left him at the dock the night before. He hoped he was wrong.

Chapter 6

July 25, 11:48 p.m.

After they talked in the infirmary, Mikie asked the nurse to show her to the lodge. She knew her way around—she herself had come to fishing camp here as a kid—but wanted to see Genevieve's reactions. They walked together along the path.

Mikie had pretty good night vision and there were no clouds. The camp—Heritage Camp, it was called—lay before them in the moonlight. It was a small camp, just a few acres, and she saw most of it on their short walk: the burly old lodge, seven A-frame cabins, a big grassy field probably used for games. The little infirmary, the basketball court, the monkey bars. Of course, she couldn't see into the woods, since all the pines and firs made them dark and deep. But she remembered them. Perfect for teenagers doing dark deeds. She could smell the lake—metallic, mossy—but couldn't see it. She could hear voices but wasn't sure which direction they came from. There was a hint of smoke in the air too. She recalled a cabin way back in the woods and wondered if it was still there and who stayed in it, if anyone.

The camp sat along Lake Sandy, the border of which formed the eastern edge of her jurisdiction and used to be stocked with rainbow trout and crappie. She vividly remembered having a barbed fishhook removed from the meat of her thumb. Her dad had used pliers to flatten the barb as much as he could before pushing the hook all the way through and out the other side. She couldn't believe he really intended to push the hook deeper, but he had explained that it would do more damage and hurt more to pull it out the way it went in. It had hurt plenty his way too.

But there was no point in thinking about her dad right now.

They stepped up onto the porch. Genevieve opened the doors, and they squeaked, then banged shut, hard. The nurse picked up a sturdy blue case from the floor, and Mikie heard pills rattling in their bottles inside.

"Do you need me for anything else?" the nurse asked. "I really need to see to the other kids."

"That's fine," Mikie said. "I'll have a look around."

"ADOPTEES ROCK!" declared a poster on the wall. A special camp for adopted kids—the idea was a little strange. A coincidence, surely, that she should be here now. Her situation was different from being adopted, of course, but if the letter she'd received a week ago was true, it meant her dad...wasn't. A man she barely remembered, a family friend she hadn't seen in decades, had just declared himself—posthumously, in his will—to be her biological father. And with that, her own family—the mom, dad, brothers she'd grown up with—looked completely different to her. She had barely had a chance to process the information, and already all her memories felt unreliable. The ground she'd built her life on felt shifty and unstable, and she had the sense of grasping for something solid. She was probably seeing signs in randomness, trying to make sense of things. She wished she could ask her mother.

But right now, she had to focus.

She looked around at the huge room. As the door squeaked and then banged shut after the nurse, a slender Asian girl in fleece pajama pants and a hooded sweatshirt emerged from a hallway to the right.

The girl's face was swollen and tear-stained, her hair wrestled into a messy knot. She was probably very pretty under normal circumstances. She startled, seeing Mikie. Mikie introduced herself. "You're a friend of Paul's?" she said. "Bad news. I'm sorry."

"Thanks," the girl said. She was hoarse. "I already know he died. Ty told me. He talked to Paul's dad."

"Do you know what happened? I'm sorry, I didn't catch your name."

"Katie. Matthews. I have no idea," she said and started to tremble. "He was standing there with Sophie? Then he was on the floor?" She started to shake her hands in front of her, as if to wake them up or shake something off them, and grimaced. "It was horrible. He didn't even look like himself."

"How awful."

"It was," Katie said, then let out a sound that resembled a whimper. She was pale, and Mikie thought the girl might pass out if she kept standing.

"Let's sit down." Katie complied, sinking to the floor. She sat on her knees, somehow making it look graceful. Mikie did the same, although her knees—a couple of decades older—cracked on the way down. "Do you know what he was doing before that?"

"Um. He played at AGT, like he always does? He plays the clarinet. He's really good, he has a scholarship for it."

"What's AGT?"

"Oh...Adoptees Got Talent. It's, like, our talent show."

"Katie, did you see him eat or drink anything unusual?"

She shook her head vigorously. She repeated what Mikie had already heard, that peanuts were off-limits, with the additional detail that the prohibition extended to all the different groups that used the facilities throughout the year. *But maybe someone had sneaked something in and eaten it*, Mikie thought. Maybe that person had played the clarinet before Paul.

"Where's his clarinet, do you suppose?" she asked.

Katie looked around, appearing a bit dazed. "I have no idea," she said. "I don't see it here. Maybe at his cabin? He didn't come straight to the dance. He was a little bit late—maybe he dropped it off first."

"Do you know if anyone else played it?"

The girl frowned. "I doubt it. I don't think anyone else knows how to play. Plus...wouldn't that be kind of gross?"

"Not any worse than kissing, I suppose," Mikie said. Casually, she asked, "Did you notice if he kissed someone?"

"Kissing's not allowed," Katie said. "Not for the campers or the counselors. Even the older ones. That just leads to problems."

Mikie raised an eyebrow. "That doesn't mean it never happens, does it? If Paul were going to kiss someone, who would it be?"

Katie eyed her for a long second before replying. "I really wouldn't know."

Mikie thanked Katie and got directions to Paul's cabin as they stood up and walked out. The young woman headed toward the woods. Mikie returned to the lodge, found the light switch, and looked over the freshly illuminated scene.

The cavernous room retained a faint impression of panic and catastrophe. A disco ball hung forgotten overhead, sending random shards of light in all directions. Drinks had been spilled, and abandoned sweatshirts and jackets slumped empty against the walls. It was obvious where the paramedics had worked on their patient: wrappers and a pair of nitrile gloves lay discarded near a smear of blood on the floor. No EpiPen. What was the blood from? She picked up the wrappers and inspected them.

Mikie had been a nurse before she got fed up with following doctors' orders (actually, she reminded herself, before she just about got herself fired for *not* following orders), so she knew what she was looking at as she perused the wrappers and plastic caps: an IV needle and line, a nasal cannula, and an endotracheal tube. So they'd started an IV and oxygen and at least attempted intubation. But it hadn't worked, she realized: the cap to a number-eleven scalpel lay on the parquet floor, and now the blood made sense to her. The ET tube couldn't pass through the swelling. The paramedics had tried a cricothyrotomy, puncturing the dying boy's throat from the outside in a last-ditch effort to get oxygen into his lungs. Perhaps it had gone in; she couldn't say. There was no tube among the detritus.

Well, no one could say the paramedics hadn't tried everything. They'd taken heroic measures—but it would have been a horrifying scene for his friends. It was probably for the best that his parents hadn't witnessed it. Resuscitation attempts could look as violent as anything, although no one complained if they worked.

No EpiPens, no cases. The paramedics would have disposed of the sharps, and perhaps they'd grabbed the EpiPens at the same time. But why wouldn't they leave the cases? Had the nurse thrown them away? Nurses, generally conscientious people, had been known to unwittingly destroy evidence at a crime scene. Not that this was a crime scene, she reminded herself. She slipped on gloves from her pocket anyway, collected everything, then turned off the lights and went outside.

It seemed darker than when she'd entered the lodge, but she knew her eyes just needed to adjust. The night air was cool and moist, and the moonlight cast long shadows from all the structures and trees.

On the front porch, she paused and considered whether to go to Paul Anderson's cabin alone. For chain of evidence, she should have another officer with her, but that was probably overkill. This might turn into a civil case, but it seemed unlikely to justify the full-court press of a homicide investigation. Still, she thought, she'd come all the way out here, so she might as well look around.

She spotted headlights on the winding road into camp; it was Jim Wu, whose arrival solved her problem. He got out of his car and headed her way. In his dark jeans and fleece jacket, he looked more like one of the camp counselors than a cop. People never took him for a cop, he'd said. Nobody sees a Chinese guy and thinks cop. He claimed this had its uses: people would say things in front of him that they wouldn't otherwise. She didn't know him very well yet, but he came highly recommended from King County, and with an impressive solve rate. She was inclined to believe him.

Just a couple of inches taller than Mikie, but much broader across the shoulders, Wu had an unusual gait—duck-footed, like a ballet dancer. She'd commented on it once and he'd surprised her by saying he'd been a ballet dancer; she had a good eye. She didn't know why he'd stopped dancing, but he kept in superlative shape.

"Well, this sucks," he said. "Nineteen-year-old kid headed off to college. Killed by a damn peanut."

"Was that confirmed?" They spoke quietly out in the open.

"More or less. They're getting some blood tests. Tryptase"—he glanced at his notes—"and histamine. They're also doing a tox screen in case he ingested something naughty. It could have been a bad asthma attack, doc said. That would be Dr. Kitchener, chief resident. However, based on the swelling and 'acuity and severity' of the attack, an allergic reaction is most likely."

"The nurse said the EpiPens didn't work."

"Doc didn't like that part. He suggested taking a look at them."

"They're not here," Mikie said. "The paramedics must have them."

"Also, the parents swear their kid would never have eaten anything that contained peanuts. He was too smart for that, hadn't done it in years."

"Supposedly no peanut products are allowed."

"Grace Chang's coming in to look at him and, as long as the family doth not protest too much, perform an autopsy. I don't like it."

"What, the autopsy?" Mikie asked. "There's no way around that."

"No, this whole thing. It just shouldn't happen."

The edge of the woods stood perhaps a hundred yards away. There was movement on one of the paths, shadows and shapes in the darkness. They could hear someone weeping—no, at least two voices, maybe more. Mikie walked in the direction of the sound, Wu following, and they found themselves on a narrow path carpeted in pine needles. In a minute or two they caught up to the sound. The woods were so dense, they didn't see the kids until they were practically on top of them. A handful of campers walked slowly amid the trees, using their phones as flashlights. One girl was being practically carried by two of her friends. Mikie spotted Genevieve bringing up the rear.

The grief of children was intense, Mikie knew. But surely for most of the kids, Paul Anderson was just one of the counselors. Summer would end. They would go back to school. This would be a sad memory.

The woods sloped gradually downward toward the lake. Mikie stopped walking and signaled for Wu to do the same, and the kids slowly disappeared into the shadows.

"Sad," she said quietly. "It's probably not going turn into a case for us, but let's do it right. Let's go look at his cabin, the two of us. Then I'll chase down this EpiPen business. You see who you can find to verify what the nurse said: that she gave him the shot in the lodge."

"You think she didn't? Or what, they were tampered with? That sounds a little far-fetched."

"If we find them and they weren't, then we're done," she said shortly. "And I'll decide what's far-fetched."

Chapter 7

July 25, 11:58 p.m.

"Excuse me." The low, distinctive voice came through the clinic window. "I'm looking for my cabin buddy."

"Hal!" Isaac said, relieved. "What's going on?"

"It was Paul," he replied. His voice was oddly thick. "Anaphylaxis. They think he might die." His diction was as crisp as ever, but with those mirrored shades Isaac couldn't tell if he'd been crying. It was hard to picture Hal crying.

"The police officer was just here. She said...well...he did die. On the way to the hospital." There was a long pause. *Maybe it would have been better not to tell him*, Isaac thought. But no. He couldn't have kept it from him.

"This is very unwelcome news," Hal finally said. "He was one of the good guys."

Was he? "I know you liked him a lot. I'm sorry, man."

Hal cleared his throat and said, "Some people are congregating at the beach. I would rather be alone in our cabin. But, per the buddy protocol, I can walk you down there first, if you want to go."

"Yeah, okay," Isaac said. He sat up and thought fast. "Give me a minute." He went to the bathroom but found the door locked from the inside. Genevieve must have locked it and forgotten; after all, she had completely forgotten him earlier. Quietly he went to the back door, hoping to find it unlocked, which it was. He stepped out lightly, walked around to the bathroom window, and wriggled in; he'd counted on fitting through, and he did. He did what he needed to do, then opened the bathroom door from the inside. He glanced in the mirror, then left the door open and joined his friend.

They walked down the path together. If Hal had noticed Isaac's convoluted route to the clinic door, he didn't say anything. "What happened, exactly?" Isaac asked.

"You missed lunch, dinner, and the dance party," Hal noted. "Are you unwell?"

"I'm okay. I had a stomachache."

They walked for a minute in silence. Then Hal said, "It happened so quickly. It was completely unexpected."

"Did you—like—see it?" Isaac was torn between curiosity and squeamishness.

"I daresay everyone present did." He stopped walking. "There was a prodigious amount of swelling...obvious respiratory distress...it was really..." Isaac waited. Hal seemed to be at a loss for words, which was unusual. But he finally said, "Terrible." He pressed his fingertips to his forehead and shuddered.

"Do you want to go back?" Isaac asked. "I don't need to go to the beach."

Hal shook his head, looking impatient. "Sophie...we need to see her."

"Why?" But Hal only walked faster.

They emerged from the forest into the bright moonlight on the sandy beach. All the older campers seemed to be there. Some girls were crying noisily, standing in a little circle and hanging onto each other. Joon and another boy stood by the waterline, skipping rocks.

Isaac counted the skips: one, two. They were throwing the stones too forcefully; instead of dancing across the water, they just slapped it and sank. The boys' faces were blank and angry in the moonlight.

Sophie was wrapped in a blanket with a friend on either side. She sat staring at nothing. Isaac felt intimidated by her grief, but Hal walked right up to her. She scrambled to stand, and he wrapped his arms around her. Isaac hung back. Sophie said something to Hal, and he replied, "That's not true." She shook her head, hard.

After that he just held her. She didn't cry, just shook and shook in his thin, hard arms.

On the way back to the cabin Isaac asked, "So what did Sophie say?"

Hal climbed into his bunk, sighed deeply, and didn't answer for a long time. Finally he said, "She said, 'Everyone I love dies.'"

Chapter 8

July 26, 1:00 a.m.

Three witnesses, Wu reported, independently swore they saw the camp nurse give Paul Anderson the EpiPen: Katie, the counselor Mikie had met in the lodge; an excitable counselor in training named Nathan; and Ty, the camp director, presumably a reliable fellow, who had headed over in his wheelchair as soon as he realized there was an emergency. Only one person, Nathan, reported seeing Paul Anderson give himself the first EpiPen, and that was because he was dancing nearby with a girl called Piper. Piper ("who's a handful, by the way," Wu commented, whatever that was supposed to mean) had confirmed the second dose but had not noticed the first.

The device was distinctive, made of bright yellow plastic, which all the witnesses had mentioned. No doubt another dozen witnesses could be found to say the same thing—everyone over twelve years old was at the dance, and no one could have missed the excitement. The stories were all consistent, and everything made sense except for one thing: the devices were missing. They weren't in the trash can, in the sharps container in the clinic, or in Genevieve's pocket or fanny pack. There was no sign of them in the plastic bin where the first aid supplies were kept, in the prescription drawer, or in the dusty corners of the lodge. Even the cases were gone. Genevieve said she simply lost track of them. "I was completely focused on Paul," she said. "I couldn't tell you about anything in that room except for him."

Wu clearly thought Mikie was crazy (though he was too respectful of her rank, or maybe just too new, to say it), but she decided to interview the paramedics while their memories were fresh.

It took dispatch a couple of minutes to locate the paramedics, who were having a snack break at the Troutdale fire station. It was 1:25 a.m. Mikie's boyfriend, Jamie, and his band, the Wrong Trousers, would be winding up their mic cords, unplugging their amps, and having a beer. Home by two. As she left camp and drove the road that followed the Sandy River to Interstate 84, she thought about driving home to intercept him. Sitting in the kitchen with a glass of cider and hearing about the gig sounded nice. *I'll do that*, she thought. But somehow her car turned right at the bridge, wended through the cute little downtown that was some city planner's idea of a tourist attraction, and headed to the firehouse. She called Jamie on the way, hoping he might answer, but she had to leave a message.

As she entered the break room, she inhaled the smell of microwave popcorn and shuddered slightly. She loathed microwave popcorn—the way it coated the roof of your mouth, the chemical flavor. A familiar face looked up as she walked in. She grinned at Frank, her brother's firefighting buddy. *Half brother*, she corrected herself, then frowned. Did she really believe that?

"Hey, Mikie. Don't look so happy to see me."

"Hey, Frank. Sorry, it's not you. How's it going?"

"I thought it was going good 'til the staties showed up. Hey, you met Melissa yet?"

"Not yet. I'm supposed to this weekend."

"Your brother's crazy about her."

"That's what I hear," she said lightly. "Is Jack around?" He nodded toward the back room. "Thanks."

"All business," he said. "You gotta play sometimes, Mikie."

This stung. Jamie had said pretty much the same thing the other day, but she tried to smile. "I play," she said. He snorted and went back to his popcorn.

The paramedics were firm: just as they'd told Wu, they hadn't removed the EpiPens. Neither had any idea where they could have gone. Mikie knew Jack slightly as an experienced paramedic, but she didn't know Juanita, who turned out to be an EMT in the process of getting more training. Juanita was positive she'd seen the EpiPens at the scene. She recalled picking up the devices to check the dose, which had been correct: 0.3 milligrams. Mainly, she said, she'd wanted to make sure it was an adult dose, not the EpiPen Jr, which contained less medication. The chambers were empty, the dose was right, and that was the last she'd thought about it.

"We were busy," she said, looking wary. "After we couldn't get the airway open, Jack tried to go in from the front. It's tricky and we were both concentrating—I'd never seen one done before."

"I'm not suggesting you should have done anything different," Mikie said. "It's just that the damn things have vanished."

"No offense, but so what?" Juanita said. "He didn't make it. That happens. Wherever the EpiPen went, it's not gonna change things for the poor guy. And his family," she added. "They were a mess." She grew quiet.

"It makes a difference to the next person," Mikie said. "If the pens were defective, maybe the whole batch is bad."

"I've never heard of that." This was Jack, the veteran paramedic. He sounded skeptical, even irritated.

"Doesn't mean it couldn't happen," Mikie said. "He did get more epinephrine later, right?"

"Of course. We followed the protocol and put it in his airway. It's faster that way, but it didn't do shit," Jack said. His face was impassive, but Mikie sensed he was more affected by the death than he wanted to appear. "There is one possibility, though." He glanced at Juanita. "Hey," he said to her, "go log the narcotics in." She opened her mouth, then closed it again. She looked mutinous but went without a word.

Mikie waited. When Jack spoke, he was looking at the table. "EpiPen training kits used to look like the real thing," he said quietly. "I didn't inspect it myself, but someone less experienced could easily mistake the old training module for an active EpiPen. It's happened before. The company eventually started to make the caps on the training kits a different color, but the old ones are still yellow. In the middle of a code it's an easy mistake to make. If someone realized they gave the wrong one, there's an incentive to hide the kit afterward. You'd get your ass handed to you on a platter."

"Would Juanita know the difference?"

"Sure, during a quiz at the office, with all the time in the world to read the labels on the side of the syringe. But in the middle of a cricothyrotomy? Not necessarily. I didn't look at the kit closely myself. I should have." He frowned.

"You gave him epi anyway. What was the delay? One minute? Two? I don't think it made a difference."

"You seem to know a lot about it," he said.

"I was a nurse," she said.

"Sounds like you still might be," he said.

"It has a way of sticking with you."

Back in her car, Mikie took a deep breath, exhaled, and dialed her dad's number. She wasn't worried about waking him—at this hour he was inevitably up, working on the project that had kept him busy for years since her mother's death: his book about Milton's daughters. But they hadn't talked much in the past month, and she wasn't ready to open the door to the conversation they both knew had to happen eventually.

"Hi, Dad."

"Hi yourself. I was just thinking about you a few minutes ago. Are you coming to the dinner on Sunday? Your brother said he and Melissa can make it."

"I don't have a lot of time," she said. "I'm on a case, and I need a favor. It's related."

"A case," he said. "Of course." He sounded completely neutral, which meant he was disappointed.

"It's not a big favor. I'd like a prescription called in. An EpiPen. Can you do that?"

"Don't you have one in your first aid kit?"

"I don't carry one anymore," she said. "That's for patrol officers."

"Why ever not? Seems like a reasonable idea to me."

"Dad. Homicide, remember? My cases are beyond first aid. Will you do it?"

"May I ask what it's for? Obviously I'll do it, but I'd like to know."

"We had a death tonight—a young person. It was an allergic reaction, and the EpiPen didn't seem to do anything."

"Well it doesn't always, if it's given too late, or incorrectly. Bees, was it?"

"Peanuts."

"Where do you want it?"

"I don't know who's open...I can call you right back."

"Don't bother. The Freddy's on Burnside is open twenty-four hours. I'll call it in there. And I hope you'll make it Sunday. I know you may feel awkward, but—"

"Thanks," she said. "Talk to you soon."

Chapter 9

July 26, 1:30 a.m.

Back in the cabin, Isaac couldn't sleep. The twins and Skater Boy Joon were somewhere else, Nathan was still at the impromptu vigil, and Hal was either asleep or doing an excellent impression of it.

Paul's bunk looked surreally empty. Someone must have come to collect his things. Had they taken his phone? Or had he kept it with him? Isaac's heart pounded. He glanced at Hal, then got up very quietly, went to Paul's bed, and felt under the mattress. There was nothing there, of course. He sat back down.

"What are you looking for?" Hal asked quietly, startling Isaac. Hal was reclining in his bunk, propped up on one elbow.

"Do you think camp will, you know, keep going?" Isaac asked. "Does everyone know what happened?"

Hal lay back down. After a long time, he said, "I have no idea."

Isaac felt keyed up and restless. He slid his sandals on. "I'm going for a walk," he said.

"Another nocturnal constitutional?" Hal's tone was ironic. "This is starting to become a habit."

"How did you—?"

"Wait," Hal said. He squinted at Isaac's foot, then pointed. "May I?" he said.

Isaac looked down at his flip-flops. "What?" He saw a brown smear. "Oh—gross."

"Give," Hal said, more insistently. He didn't wait, but swiped the shoe off Isaac's foot in one swift move.

"Hey!" Isaac shouted. "Why?"

Hal wiped at the brown smear with his index finger, sniffed it, and touched it carefully to his tongue.

Isaac couldn't help gagging. "That is disgusting!"

"Not at all," Hal said. He slipped on a headlamp, which looked really strange combined with the shades.

"Don't those sort of cancel each other out?" Isaac asked.

"On the contrary, the one makes the other tolerable."

"Why did you put that in your mouth?"

"Because," he said, "this is not a simple case of shit-shoe, Isaac. Your shoe is smeared with peanut butter."

Isaac stared. "That's not possible."

"Nevertheless. You try it."

"No way." But he did sniff at it, cautiously. It smelled of peanuts— and chocolate. On closer inspection, there were two shades of brown smeared together. "But where did it come from?"

"We should retrace your steps."

They walked from their cabin to the infirmary. The air was cool and alive with insect song. No one seemed to be out, although a light shone from a window in the lodge.

Hal headed for the main door of the infirmary.

"No," Isaac said, "I went to the bathroom first." They walked back in that direction, lights trained on the ground to reveal dirt, pine nee-dles, a hair clip, and a folded-up piece of paper that turned out to be a game of hangman for which the solution was "Game of Thrones."

Hal whispered, "Where did you go next?"

"To the beach, with you. No, wait! I went through the window."

"You came out the back door."

"But I went in through the window first, because I needed the bathroom and it was locked. Then I went out through the door." They stepped carefully around the clinic to a small window, which stood open. On the other side was the bathroom, which Isaac knew had two doors: one led to the nurse's bedroom, the other to the infirmary. Either door might have been open. He hoped Genevieve wasn't awake to hear them. In any case, there was nothing under the window.

"Nothing," Isaac said. "Hal? What are you doing?"

The other boy stood very still. He licked a finger and held it up to the air, then took a few steps toward the woods. Following the wind? There wasn't much.

The wind hadn't taken it very far. They found the peanut butter cup wrapper about fifty yards away, a smidge of crushed candy still adhered to the inside.

Isaac and Hal sat on the dock in the moonlight, lake water lapping at the pylons just below their dangling feet. They had found only the one candy wrapper and nothing more.

"Should we tell someone?" Isaac asked for maybe the third time.

"Not at present. I'm thinking."

"Could it have been the pies? Maybe someone smushed it into the bottom of one."

"Perhaps." Hal stood up and the two of them walked back to the firepit. There were no pie tins—nothing but the damp ashes of last night's fire.

"Or maybe it was an accident," Isaac said. He hoped so, but he didn't say that.

"Also possible," Hal said shortly.

"Well, who eats peanut butter cups? Tanya loves candy. Remember she said she's addicted?"

"Isaac."

"What?"

"Do you ever allow yourself the luxury of an unexpressed thought?"

"Sorry."

"I didn't mean to be rude. I'm trying to think."

"That's okay. I'm going to go back. I'll let you think."

Isaac headed back up the path, feeling restless and a little spooked.

It must have been an accident, he thought. *It probably happened all the time.* That didn't help. Everything seemed somehow potent: the cool, damp air, the shards of moonlight on the dark water. Pine needles gave way, sliding under his feet as he walked.

As he neared the infirmary, he heard people talking. He recognized Sophie's voice and stopped walking. He could see her now, with her mother. Their backs were to him, and Genevieve's posture was one of supplication. He wanted nothing more than to disappear, but then Sophie fainted. Without thinking, he ran up to help.

Chapter 10

July 26, 1:15 a.m.

After the vigil, Genevieve insisted that Sophie return to the nurse's cabin with her for the night. Sophie didn't resist. She let her mother test her blood sugar, which was high at 280—no doubt due to stress. "Let me do your insulin, honey," she said.

Sophie didn't reply but got up and limped to the fridge. She drew up her insulin, looking pale and expressionless in the fluorescent light from the fridge.

"Let me, honey," Genevieve said. She guided Sophie back to bed and prepared her skin for the shot. Sophie lay silent and unflinching as the little needle went in. Once, she had been a small girl, soft and yielding, a sweet-smelling baby with enormous brown eyes. That was before she became a prickly teenager with moods and colored contact lenses. Genevieve kissed her daughter's head.

"Mom?"

"I'm here, sweetie."

"How could this happen?"

"I don't know."

Sophie closed her eyes—green today—without taking off her clothes or even removing her prosthesis, but it wouldn't do any harm for one night. Genevieve felt completely wrung out, shaking with fatigue. When she closed her eyes, she saw that poor boy's face and heard the whistling sound of his attempts to get air through a throat that was quickly swelling shut. When the music was turned off it had been loud—so loud.

But it had eventually stopped.

She couldn't sleep. Thank God Sophie seemed to be resting, at least. She had withdrawn, but Genevieve would call it rest, not catatonia.

Just as she was starting to think that perhaps sleep would come, her daughter bolted upright. "Mom," she said. Genevieve turned on the bedside light. Sophie's eyes were glassy. "I can't breathe," she said. "Mom. I can't breathe." She was panting.

Genevieve took Sophie's damp hand, but she snatched it away. "Close your mouth," Genevieve instructed. "Breathe on a count of three. In and out."

"I can't!" Sophie said wildly. "I can't be in here." Before Genevieve could stop her, Sophie was up and moving to the door. Then she was out in the night air, and Genevieve was running to keep up.

"Sophie, wake up!" she whisper-shouted and grabbed her daughter's hand again. It was damp and trembling finely. She found Sophie's pulse with her index finger; it was fast—too fast—and thready. *Night terrors*, Genevieve thought. It had been years. Sophie thought she was awake, but she wasn't. It was a miracle she didn't walk into doors and walls, but her eyes seemed to work during these spells.

"It was my fault," Sophie said clearly. "Mom?"

Genevieve felt like her insides were collapsing.

"Sophie. You're asleep. This is a dream. Come back inside, now."

"No! It was my fault. My fault, my fault." She was speaking rapidly, in a normal volume. Genevieve glanced around.

"Honey, nothing is your fault. Come inside."

"I didn't mean it!" Sophie wailed. She looked all around. Searching for something. Then, quietly, "Mom? I didn't mean it." Sophie collapsed suddenly, as though all her bones had softened.

"Sophie!" Genevieve caught her awkwardly around the waist. She might have dropped her, or might have fallen herself, but help emerged from the darkness. It was Isaac; he must have been in the infirmary all day and night—she'd completely forgotten about him. He looked worried. "Help me get her inside," she said, and he came forward and took hold of Sophie's legs. Together they got Sophie inside and onto the first bed. Isaac switched on the light.

Sophie looked terrible—her skin was white, but her cheeks were flushed, and her eyes were half-closed. She grabbed a stethoscope and listened to Sophie's heart. It was beating too fast, close to 150 beats per minute. "Hand me that cuff," she instructed Isaac and took her blood pressure with trembling hands. It was 170/100. So why did Sophie faint, if not from low blood pressure? She pulled the O$_2$ monitor out of a nearby drawer and clipped it to Sophie's finger. Her oxygen saturation was perfect at 100 percent.

She knew what she would do if this was someone else's child: wait a few minutes, monitor her vitals, and see if she came around. Her color was already looking a bit better. But it was hard not to panic. She wanted to call an ambulance. No, not another ambulance at camp! Maybe she could drive to Emanuel herself, it wasn't far. Adventist was even closer.

"What did you hear, Isaac?" she asked, trying to distract herself.

"Nothing," the boy said softly. She knew he was shy. He often looked as though he wished no one could see him. He gestured to the front of the clinic. "The door..." He looked embarrassed. *Of course,* she thought. The door banged shut if you didn't watch it.

"Right. Sorry for waking you."

"That's okay. Um, can I do anything?"

"Stand here for a sec while I grab something." She hurried to her bedroom and retrieved the blood-sugar monitor. When she poked her daughter's finger with the lancet, Sophie pulled back and grimaced. That was good; she was responsive. But her blood sugar was still high at 330, although she hadn't eaten anything for hours. "Damn it," she said.

"Is that bad?" Isaac asked.

"It's only been a couple of hours since the last dose," she muttered before realizing she shouldn't be talking to Isaac about this. In fact, he shouldn't even be here. "Isaac, would you mind getting Ty? I need to tell him I might have to go to the hospital."

"Sure."

"Do you know where his room is?" she asked.

He nodded and went out the door. Even hurrying, he didn't let it bang shut. Considerate kid. In about two minutes, the assistant director, Katie, came through the same door in her pajamas, looking like she hadn't slept. Isaac was right behind her.

"What's up?" she gasped. "Ty's asleep. Do you need me?"

"I might need to take Sophie to the hospital."

"Oh no. Is she in shock? What happened?"

Genevieve turned back to the pale girl lying on the bed. "Sophie? Sweetie pie? Can you wake up?"

Her eyes opened. She rubbed her face with pale hands. "Mom?"

"I'm here. You had a bad dream."

"It was a dream?" Sophie's eyes widened and she sat up.

"Well. Not all of it. It was an awful night. But you're okay now."

Sophie's eyes flickered back and forth, reading her mother's face. "Paul?"

"Paul's gone, sweetie. I'm so sorry."

"Oh my God," she said and fell back. She pressed her face into the pillow and screamed. Even muffled, it was a horrifying sound.

Chapter 11

July 26, 7:00 a.m.

Jamie had been asleep when Mikie got home, and he was still asleep when she left. She kissed his hair and he half-woke, groping for her hand and smiling. "You smell funny," she whispered. "It's rock 'n' roll," he murmured.

"It's the inside of that disgusting band van," she pointed out. "Plus"—she stopped to sniff the air around him—"a half-decent IPA."

"What I said. Rock 'n' roll."

Mikie's phone rang and she answered it on the way out the door. She was headed for the station, hoping to review all the information that had come in overnight before the autopsy started—it would begin at either eight or eleven in the morning, depending on what else Grace Chang had going on. She hadn't gotten enough sleep, but that was normal during the beginning of an investigation; insomnia was typical until her questions were answered. She just wished she'd had a chance to talk to Jamie about everything.

"Hello there," an unfamiliar voice said. "This is Dr. Kitchener at Emanuel. I'm not sure who I'm calling, but Officer Wu left this number? It's regarding Paul Anderson."

The voice was male, about her age, and hesitant. "That's fine, Doctor, thanks for calling. I'm Sergeant O'Malley and it's my case along with Detective Wu. What's on your mind?"

"I'm just getting ready to go home—long night—and I was going through my labs and thought I better let somebody know. This is a really terrible case, isn't it? We haven't lost a patient to anaphylaxis in years. So, anything unexpected kind of jumps out at you."

"What's unexpected?"

"We did a number of labs on the boy's arrival and, for the most part, the results are consistent with anaphylaxis. I don't know how much detail you want?"

"Pretend you're talking to a nurse," she suggested.

"O...kay. Well, we look at histamine levels, which tell you about the extent of the allergy, and his were stratospheric, which is expected. High levels of tryptase—that's a respiratory enzyme that's very high in respiratory failure—also expected. Peanut antigen positive."

"So, what is it that bothers you?"

"Well, he had hypoglycemia—low blood sugar. Definitely not expected. The finger stick was done en route and it was low, but I thought it might be a false reading. Water or sweat on the strip or the ambulance bouncing around can throw things off. I don't take finger stick readings too seriously in the field. But the serum reading—the official result, if you will—was even lower."

"How low? And why is that a problem?"

"It was sixty-five milligrams per deciliter in the ambulance, but it was forty in our hospital. Forty! Normal is over seventy. It just doesn't make sense. The body is stressed to the max in anaphylaxis. Blood sugar goes crazy—but crazy high, not low."

"I see."

"And then there's the fact that his catecholamine levels were normal—that's epinephrine and the like—and they should have been high if he actually got two doses."

She decided it couldn't hurt to ask. "Doctor, you didn't see the EpiPens, did you? Either one of them? They've gone missing."

"I'd say they were missing from the get-go. I don't believe he ever got an EpiPen." He didn't sound hesitant now.

"His blood sugar was low and his epinephrine was normal, right? What if he got an insulin pen instead of an EpiPen?"

"I didn't think of that, but it makes sense." He sounded impressed. "Except that they look quite different. The EpiPen is—"

"Yellow, right," she said. "Thanks for calling. If those results are ready, our pathologist will want to look them over."

"Sure, okay. You might ask them to check the insulin level. I didn't think of that last night, unfortunately."

She called Grace, who was nearly ready to do the autopsy. Then she called Wu. "I don't want to miss the autopsy, but one of us needs to get back to camp."

"If you say so. What am I looking for?"

"The missing EpiPens. Failing that, an insulin pen. Failing that, just try to piss people off and see what happens."

"My specialty."

Chapter 12

July 26, 8:00 a.m.

Isaac was on a pirate ship. Monopoly money was blowing around in every direction, flying overboard and clogging up the lake. Sophie was crying and pleading with him. "Let me explain," she said, but instead of explaining, she took off her clothes, dropped her prosthetic leg on the dock, and dragged him overboard. The water was cold, making him gasp and choke; he struggled to swim, but she had hold of his arms, teasing; sodden dollar bills surrounded his face, he couldn't breathe, couldn't make her understand that he was drowning. Then someone hauled him into a kayak, and little Eliza was flying overhead with butterfly wings, dodging arrows and yelling, "They work! They really work!" Sophie and Genevieve were busy doing CPR on someone lying on the deck in a pool of murky water; he couldn't see the person's face, but when Sophie looked up and saw Isaac, she said, "I didn't mean it." Someone shouted, "Isaac!"

He sat up, gasping, to find Hal standing over him, arms folded.

"Are you quite all right?"

"What the hell?" Isaac said, feeling sweaty and freaked out. "Were you watching me sleep?"

One eyebrow appeared over the shades. "Hardly. I was attempting to wake you up. We're about to miss breakfast."

"Oh. Thanks."

"You're welcome."

Isaac supposed he wasn't used to having friends. "Sorry—bad dream."

"So I surmised." Hal held the door for him.

It was a glum and half-empty lodge this morning. Some campers had probably slept in, but some were gone and some were in the process of leaving, carrying their duffel bags and Pillow Pets to the parking area, hugging their friends goodbye, and shedding tears. From C Cabin, only Skater Boy was leaving.

Ty wheeled to the front of the room and looked around, his expression solemn. Already subdued, the campers fell silent. Kids twisted in their seats to look at him, waiting. Some looked hopeful, some anxious. *What could he say that could possibly make it better?* Isaac wondered.

"My friends," Ty said. He looked at the campers in turn. His eyes were intense, filled with light. Isaac noticed, not for the first time, the acne scars that marred his round face. "We lost a good man last night. I just want to say one thing, Heritage Camp. The counselors are here for you. We love you. Be strong. And we'll find some way"—he stopped abruptly and choked out the rest—"to honor Paul."

Some campers applauded. Someone sobbed. One of the little kids piped up, "What happened?"

Nathan sighed and pushed his food around.

"You are, uncharacteristically, picking at your food," Hal said.

"This is like the worst thing that's ever happened here," Nathan said. "Maybe the worst thing ever, period. I just can't believe it." His eyes filled with tears.

"Indeed," Hal said. "Do we know how it happened?"

Unexpectedly, Nathan let out a sob. In his peripheral vision, Isaac noticed heads whipping around to look their way. "Be cool," Isaac murmured. "Sorry, it's just—people are staring."

"Who cares?" Hal asked. Isaac blushed but realized it wasn't a reprimand. He really didn't know who would care.

"I'm sorry!" Nathan said. "It's just...I think maybe I do know what happened. And it's horrible."

"You have a hypothesis?" Hal asked.

Nathan nodded.

"Let's discuss," Hal said quietly. "But are people, in fact, staring?"

"Yes," Isaac said.

"In that case, not here."

They scraped their plates into the bin and stowed them in the rack. At the door, Hal stopped and looked around, scanning the tables behind them before going out. They emerged into the sun. The morning was bright, but there was a bank of dark clouds to the east, toward the coast. Hal walked to the boathouse, and the other two boys followed.

"We're going boating?" Nathan asked.

"Alternative venue. The middle of the lake is a good place for a private conversation."

They worked together to move the two-man canoe into the water, then Isaac dragged a small green kayak into the shallows beside it. He liked kayaking, although he wanted a bit of distance, too; Hal was much too observant. He didn't want to sit face-to-face in the canoe. In the kayak, he could turn away or look down at the water.

"We need life jackets," Nathan said, handing them out.

They paddled out for three or four minutes. "I think this is adequate," Hal said, looking around. "Sound carries well across water, so do modulate your voices."

"Modulating," Isaac said. "What happened, Nathan?"

"Well. I mean, I don't know for sure. But do you remember that news story about the girl who died because her boyfriend ate peanut butter cereal, like, four hours earlier? And they kissed? No? You guys never heard about this?" They shook their heads. "Well, I think that's probably what happened. And I left them alone. If I had only stayed down there...they wouldn't have done it and he'd still be here." His eyes filled with tears.

"Someone ate peanut butter cereal and kissed Paul?" Isaac asked.

"I don't know about cereal. But there was kissing. Down at the firepit, after the talent show."

"Who was he kissing?" Isaac asked, trying to sound casual.

"Isaac," Hal said, "why ask a question when the answer is bound to distress you?"

"I don't know what you're talking about," Isaac said, but he knew he was blushing furiously. "And who talks like that?"

"There is nothing wrong with the way I talk. Per *Webster's Third New International Dictionary*, the English language contains more than four hundred and seventy thousand words. It allows for great precision. It isn't my fault the vast, unimaginative majority use the same two thousand over and over again."

"Sorry," Isaac said as remorse warmed his face. He finally had a friend, and he couldn't understand why he was suddenly picking on him.

"No need to apologize. Unrequited love has made many a better man testy."

"Sophie and Paul go way back," Nathan said unhappily. "She must be feeling so awful."

"Nathan. Sophie wouldn't make such an elementary mistake. Isaac is infatuated with her—"

"I am not!"

"Dude, you are," Nathan said.

"Well, nobody knows that," Isaac said.

"If by nobody, you mean everybody," Nathan said. But he smiled, just a bit.

"As I was saying. Isaac appreciates Sophie's more superficial characteristics, and it's understandable that he, as well as most people confronted with the razzle-dazzle of her appearance, tends to overlook her intelligence. But she is, in fact, a very smart person who knows better than to accidentally expose a peanut-allergic individual to a Reese's Cup."

"Razzle-dazzle?" Nathan said.

Accidentally? Isaac thought. He took a deep breath and paddled on one side, trying to avert his face. Unfortunately, he only succeeded in turning in a circle. Hal's mirrored gaze confronted him again.

"What are you thinking, Isaac?" he asked.

"What? Nothing, why? I mean, Reese's Cup?" He hadn't known they were going to share information with Nathan.

"That was merely a hypothetical example," Hal said pointedly.

"Oh."

"Nathan, Sophie didn't kill Paul. Don't give it another thought—and don't mention it to anyone else."

"How can you be so sure?" Isaac blurted. "I mean..."

"It's perfectly simple. I know her."

Isaac glanced at Nathan and was surprised to see him looking back. He realized they must have both had doubts about Sophie. "If you say so," Isaac said.

"Should you perhaps get back to your CIT duties?" Hal asked Nathan.

"I guess so. I haven't seen the twins today...maybe they went home, although they weren't on the list."

"Or maybe that's them right there," Isaac said, nodding at the shore. From the middle of the lake they had a clear view of Max and David, one twin on the other's shoulders, staggering around behind the girls' shower building. It looked like they were trying to see through the high windows.

"Oh my God," Nathan said. "Paddle faster!"

When they landed at the dock Nathan took off running toward the twins. Seeing Nathan approach at top speed, the one on the bottom—there was no telling them apart at a distance—started and staggered, and they both went down in a tangle of limbs. As awful as things were, Isaac couldn't help smiling.

"Can he handle those two?"

"I believe his confidence is improving," Hal said.

Chapter 13

July 26, 10:00 a.m.

Mikie didn't mind autopsies—not really. The dead couldn't suffer. The hard part was talking to the bereaved. She felt their pain, sometimes as a physical presence: a catch in the chest, a headache that nagged for the duration of a case. Once she had a sore throat for three weeks, which resolved when they arrested a rapist who throttled his victims.

The only problem with autopsies was that sometimes they were gross. This one was just sad.

"You can see how the pupils are fixed and dilated," Grace was saying. She was Mikie's favorite pathologist, and a friend. They sometimes went out to shows together—she was a fan of the Wrong Trousers. A tattoo of a hula girl playing the stand-up bass adorned her flank, which of course was routinely hidden by her professional clothing. Her Jimmy Choo shoes sat outside the door, where she'd swapped them for the dumpy brown clogs she used at work. "Sweat is dried all over. There are two tiny puncture wounds in the right quadriceps—well-developed quadriceps, which I mention because there's only the remotest chance the epi was diverted to the fatty tissue and didn't get into the bloodstream in time. I took a biopsy of the site to make sure."

"Can you call the cause of death?"

"Not quite yet. Well, respiratory arrest is safe to say. Secondary to what, though, is the question."

"Is there any question?"

"That he was in anaphylaxis? No. You saw the airway—super edematous. Yikes. But that doesn't mean that's what caused the arrest. From the way it looks, it seems the heart stopped first—cardiac arrest led to respiratory arrest. Normally it's the other way around. There are inconsistencies."

"The blood sugar?"

"That is a bugaboo, isn't it? The sweat and the pupils also don't match. We see that in hypoglycemia, not in anaphylaxis. Almost nobody dies of hypoglycemia anymore, though. I know you wanted an insulin level, but it just can't be done postmortem. Emanuel can't do it on last night's blood either, not this far out. I have another idea, though."

"What?"

"Do you mind if I check it out first? It might sound stupid."

"Of course I mind! No secrets."

"Oh, fine, you bossy cow."

Mikie grinned. "That's Sergeant Cow to you."

"Give me a minute, at least." Grace bent to her microscope. For a few minutes, she just looked, turning the little knobs on the viewfinder, toying with the focus. "How's Jamie, anyway?"

"Asleep. He had a late gig last night. At least he got to sleep in."

"How do you guys ever see each other?"

"We don't."

"Secret to a great relationship?"

Mikie forced a laugh. "Maybe." She realized she still hadn't spoken to him about her dad, or much of anything really, in a couple of days.

"Christ on a bicycle," Grace said. "I had a feeling."

"What?"

"Come and look. See the crystals?"

"What am I looking at?"

"This is the biopsy I was telling you about. How did you get to be a sergeant when you don't even listen?"

The image under the scope was quite beautiful. It looked like a landscape from another planet, or the deep ocean. "Is this the injection site?"

"Yes, right between the two punctures. They're really close together. And that's not epi you're looking at. Someone gave this boy a shot, all right—a shot of insulin."

Chapter 14

July 26, 9:30 a.m.

Isaac and Hal stowed the boats, cooperating wordlessly, and started up the path.

"So what do you think happened?" Isaac asked.

"Did you notice who was missing at breakfast?"

"You mean besides half of camp?"

"Yes. Someone whose absence is conspicuously inappropriate."

"Um, okay...who?"

"Someone whose services might be needed in a crisis? Come now, Isaac." He tapped one foot impatiently.

Light dawned all at once. "Tanya Miller," Isaac said. "Maybe she's sick."

"Was she in the infirmary last night?"

"Not when I was there."

"Does she seem likely to allow a minor illness to keep her away from campers in severe emotional distress?"

"I guess not," Isaac said.

"Is her car here? Never mind, you wouldn't have checked. The answer is yes. So where is she? Never mind that, either. She's in her cabin."

"But what about the fire? I thought she was supposed to move out."

"Isaac, did you get the staff directory? The one that came in the post before camp?"

Isaac was having trouble following the conversation. He figured "post" probably meant mail. "I think so." They were at their cabin now.

"I require a copy. Would you be willing to lend me yours?"

"I don't think I brought it...oh, wait, I did." Michelle had strongly recommended it. *The more faces you can match with names*, she'd said, *the less anxious you'll feel*. But he had been unconcerned with the staff, so he hadn't even opened it. It was the other campers that worried him. They went into the cabin, and Hal went straight to the case where he padlocked his PC. He typed in the incredibly long password ("No, passphrase, far safer," he'd said) that let him into his top-secret programs. Whatever he was working on ("for Intel, can't be too careful"), he was paranoid about security.

"What do you want it for?"

"Just a little theory I'm working with. Genotypes and phenotypes."

"Of course," Isaac said. "Why not? Everyone else is."

Hal turned and looked at him. "They are? Who? What have you heard?"

"Nothing, man. I was kidding."

"I see. Good." Then he said, "Damn. The connection's been terminated."

Isaac rifled through his luggage. He couldn't find the directory at first, then remembered he'd zipped it in a front pocket along with the journal he hadn't cracked open yet. "Just give it a minute," he said. He tossed the book to Hal, who caught it in one hand without looking. Nathan called this type of ability "judo magic."

"When it's up at all, it's positively glacial," Hal said. He sighed deeply. "I'm out of patience. Let's go boost the signal."

"How are we supposed to do that?" But Hal didn't answer. He just glanced at Isaac, stood up, and stretched. Then he locked his laptop up again, tucking the staff directory in with it.

"Follow me if you're curious." They walked to the main lodge. Isaac hesitated at the swinging doors that led to the kitchen, but Hal went right in and spoke to the chef. She was a white-haired, sizeable lady referred to as "that battle-axe" by Nathan, and Isaac was a little afraid of her. "Good morning, Janet. May I have a sizeable piece of aluminum foil, please? It's for a project."

Chef Janet beamed at him. Isaac couldn't believe it. He had never seen her smile—not once.

"Sure thing, dear."

"I thank you."

"Anytime. You want something else? I got cookies. They're warm."

"Well, in that case..." Hal accepted a small stack of chocolate chip cookies that smelled heavenly and practically oozed chocolate.

"Some milk?"

"Thank you, no, we're on a schedule."

"Come anytime, dear. You're always welcome. And your friend here."

"Thanks," Isaac said. He found the big woman's friendliness alarming. They left through the swinging doors and reentered the cavernous main room. "What was that all about?" he whispered.

Hal chewed and swallowed. "Oh, my. Warm cookies. Quite literally, I built the woman a better mousetrap. Plagued with rodents, she was. Anyway, the Wi-Fi's in the broom closet. We'll go quietly." He glanced at Isaac. "Close your mouth, Isaac, you're gawping."

Isaac closed his mouth and tried for dignity. "You, you just—how? A mousetrap?"

"Have a cookie and concentrate. See if there's anyone in the hall."

Isaac took a bite—it was incredible—and said, "Fine, but later on, you're going to explain."

He peered around the corner. Empty.

They exited the main room through a doorway on the left and walked into an empty hallway Isaac had never seen. The screeching sound of a fax machine startled him, and he backpedaled a bit. The noise was coming from an open doorway, which Isaac realized was the camp office. He'd always come the other way, through the door from the kitchen. Hal placed a finger to his lips and pointed at a closed door. It was a broom closet, containing a mop and bucket and some other cleaning supplies. He jerked his head toward Isaac, who ducked inside.

It smelled of both pine trees and chemicals. The mop tickled Isaac's neck, and he batted it away. Hal came in behind him, pushing past him to the corner. But there was nothing there except a few holes in the wall, about the right size for a couple of cables. Hal whispered, "The router used to be right here." It was dark, but light shone through the holes. Isaac could see Hal's silhouette as he removed his sunglasses, bent his head, and peered through the opening.

"What is it?" Isaac whispered.

"They moved it into the office. I can see it."

Isaac could just reach the other hole. He recognized Katie in the room next door. She was doing something hurriedly with the fax machine, tearing out a piece of paper that must have gotten jammed. She turned the machine off and on again, then headed to the door. But then she changed her mind, turned around, and picked up a notebook. On her way out, she stopped and stared at the wall, and Isaac had the impression that she could see him looking back. But the closet was dark, and he hoped it was his imagination that pinned her gaze to his face.

Then she left. Isaac exhaled. He hadn't realized he was holding his breath.

"That was scary," he whispered. Hal put his shades back on and nodded.

The door opened. Isaac froze, positive he was about to see Katie frowning in at him.

But he had to look down to see who was speaking.

"Gentlemen," Ty said. He smiled broadly. "Time to come out of the closet."

An hour later, Isaac and Hal were back in their cabin. "I'm not gay," Isaac said. Again. "I like girls. Not you, not Ty."

"Obviously."

But it seemed to Isaac that Hal hadn't tried very hard to convince Ty, whose broad grin hinted that they'd sought out the broom closet for privacy.

And Hal didn't even mention their plan to improve the internet speed—although somehow, in those awkward moments after Ty found them, he'd managed to bring the conversation around to the lagginess problem and had even gotten into the office to boost the signal. And they hadn't been expelled from camp. Isaac supposed that was the main thing. But Ty's smile still embarrassed him.

Worse, Ty had asked Isaac to stay behind a moment. "I remembered who you remind me of!" he'd said cheerfully. "Check this out. Any relation?" And he'd handed over a camp photo from two years earlier. He'd even circled the face he wanted Isaac to see, just to make sure there was no mistake. His smile had looked sincere, and Isaac really had no idea what his intentions were. He folded up the photo and stuck it in his back pocket, shoving it down as deep as it would go.

Now, Isaac left Hal tapping away happily at his laptop and found a nice tree to climb. Up there, he breathed easier. People, he had found, rarely looked up, even when they were looking for you. Which no one was—not today. Supervision at Heritage Camp had become slightly lackadaisical, as his mother would say, at least for the older campers.

From his vantage point, he figured he was probably the first person to see the police car wending its way down the country road that led to camp. *They know about the video*, he thought for no reason. No, that was silly. It was probably just follow-up stuff. Routine. His heart beat anxious wings in his chest. Where would they go first?

He wished he knew where Sophie was. He was fairly certain she and her mom hadn't gone to the hospital last night after all; he would have heard the car. And she'd been coming around by the time he left the infirmary.

He could still hear it in his mind—the awful way she'd screamed when she realized it hadn't all been a dream.

Making a quick decision, he shimmied down the tree and walked—casually, he hoped—to the infirmary. He found Genevieve sitting at her desk looking stressed, rummaging in her top drawer.

"Isaac!" she said. "Oh my gosh. It's been so crazy—I wanted to apologize for forgetting about you yesterday. I think I even left you in the dark last night!"

"It's okay," he said. "I was fine. Really."

"Do you have everything you need now?"

"Yeah. Well, except...could I get a couple more ibuprofen?"

"Sure." The drawer closed with a metallic snap, and she stood up and dispensed a couple of the orange tablets. She looked tired. He wanted to ask her about Sophie, but the right words eluded him. Finally, he just blurted out, "Is Sophie okay?"

"She's fine," Genevieve said quickly. Her gaze flickered to the bathroom door, and Isaac knew somehow that Sophie was in there. "Thanks for your help last night. She just...well, I'm not going to say any more about it. Just—thanks for helping us. It was an awful day. Now. What about you? Stomachache better?"

"Good. Yeah, no worries here. Just want to make sure it doesn't come back."

"Okay. Come see me anytime."

"Knock, knock." A man stood at the front door, sticking his head in. He was a slight, fit-looking Asian man, and Isaac thought he was someone from Heritage; then he spotted the gun in a black holster at the man's hip. The other police officer, the woman with the glasses, wasn't with him. "Sorry to interrupt," the man said cheerfully.

Genevieve frowned. Lines appeared around her mouth. "Can I help you? I'm with a camper, as you can see."

"I'm good," Isaac said and got up. He thought about the candy wrapper and found he suddenly had to swallow hard. He finished his paper cup of water and headed to the door. On his way out, he had to pass the policeman, who was looking at him with interest.

Genevieve said, "Are you sure, Isaac? Because this can wait, no doubt."

"Won't take long," the policeman said. He flashed Isaac a quick smile that looked friendly but somehow wasn't. "You can come back in a few."

Isaac nodded and slipped past the man into the entryway. He thought he'd sit on the plastic chair there, but when the man closed the door he realized he wouldn't hear anything that way. The windows were open, though. He crumpled the empty cup that was still in his hand and stepped quietly out the front door. He sat in the porch swing; it moved beneath him in an unsettling way. He strained to hear the conversation inside but caught only the faint sound of voices, so he got up and walked along the side of the building until he was at the side window.

"...breaks the rules," the cop was saying.

"What are you talking about?" Genevieve sounded irritated.

"Well, this helpful sticker right here says food and drugs are not to be mixed in the refrigerator. I count one turkey sandwich, three cartons of orange juice, and about a hundred little vials of something or other. U100, U500...what's that stuff?"

"I'm sorry, your point is what? Are you from Jayco?"

"Say Jay what? No, ma'am. I'm just trying to be helpful. This sticker's probably been here so long you forgot to read it. Rules are rules, though. Sometimes when people are sloppy with the little things, it means they might be sloppy with the big things too."

Genevieve sounded outraged. "Are you trying to be insulting? What does my refrigerator have to do with anything? Is this even about Paul?"

"Anyone here use an insulin pen?"

The nurse took so long to reply that Isaac thought he'd missed her answer. He heard the hinges of her chair squeak as she sat down heavily. When she finally spoke, she sounded angry.

"Is that your theory? That I gave the poor boy an insulin pen by mistake? Where on earth—hello, Ty, do you need something?"

Isaac froze; he'd missed Ty's arrival somehow. He wondered if the director had spotted him sitting still beneath the window.

"Sorry to interrupt," Ty's voice said humbly. "Do you have an ACE wrap? Elbow-sized?"

"Does someone need me? I don't mind heading out there. This can wait."

"No need. Just some TLC."

The door banged shut again, and Isaac scrambled away behind the building. He heard the cop say, "Who uses the insulin?" Once Isaac was at the back of the infirmary he stood up, brushing leaves off his shorts. He turned and started, seeing a face at the darkened window of the nurse's quarters. Big blue eyes stared from the window, and pink and green braids hung around the lovely face taut with misery. Sophie held her palm flat against the window screen, looking right at him.

Chapter 15

July 26, 12:10 p.m.

"Hal. The cops are here again."

"Mm." His friend sat staring, through red wraparound sunglasses, at his laptop. There was no doubt he was enjoying the blazing new internet speed.

"If we're going to tell them about the wrapper, this would be the time, man."

"Mm." He didn't look up.

"Well, are we?"

His fingers flew across the keyboard. "One minute," he said. Then, "Look at this."

Isaac leaned in tentatively. Hal had the annoying habit of snatching his laptop out of view as soon as anything interesting appeared. He claimed he was afraid of competitors getting a look at his program, but Isaac suspected he did a fair amount of surfing. But this time he turned the screen to make it easier to read.

Qualitative studies (unpublished)—carried out between January and April 2014 in situ in Bangkok through questionnaires and private oral interviews—contradict the Royal Thai government's assertion that strict precautions have always been taken to prevent those in the adoption business from trafficking in children. Subjects in this study complained of waking up to find that their babies had been taken from their homes or, in one case, from the woman's hospital room a day after birth; of being subjected to harassment and threats of violence from criminal gangs; and of being forced to accept payment in cash or drugs in exchange for their children, then being threatened with exposure for baby selling and/or narcotic use, crimes for which the penalties are harsh in Thailand. (Capital punishment is permitted for certain drug-related crimes.)

In addition, there are nine independent case studies described by Miller et al. which, taken together, confirm that at least some mothers were deprived of their infants through deceit or coercion during the 1990s and early 2000s in Bangkok. At the time, all of the subjects in these studies worked as "hostesses" or "bar girls": both terms are often used as euphemisms for commercial sex work. Although none of the women self-identified as sex workers, "hostesses" can be considered a similarly marginalized and vulnerable demographic. Ethnicity also seems to have been a factor: seven women were of Khmer origin and one was of Hmong origin. The ninth mother's ethnicity was unspecified "hill tribe."

"Okay," Isaac said, "so, wow. Horrible and interesting."

"Is that all?"

"What else is there to say?"

"This doesn't suggest anything to you? I mean, as a normal person."

Isaac wasn't sure which one of them was supposed to be normal, but he said, "That once upon a time, people stole babies from poor women in Thailand. Like I said, horrible."

"And that's really all you get from this?" Hal asked. Then he winced. "Sorry, that was rude. I'm wondering if I'm making too quantum a leap here. I would appreciate your perspective."

"I don't know," Isaac said. The whole subject made him feel squirmy. "Maybe. I know it says the '90s and 2000s and that's when we were born, but they're not talking about me. I know all about my birth mother. I even have a picture. And Heritage wasn't involved in that stuff. That's why my parents chose them. 'Ethical, child-centered adoptions' and all that."

"Thanks," Hal said and turned back to the screen. "That helps."

"Are you saying I'm wrong? Should I be getting something else here?"

"Well, one of us is wrong," Hal said brightly. "But don't be alarmed. It's entirely possible that it's me."

Isaac had a strong feeling he didn't mean it.

Chapter 16

July 26, 1:00 p.m.

Once the death was officially suspicious, Mikie moved quickly. A team of uniformed officers was dispatched to Heritage Camp to search for the missing EpiPens, and a newbie officer was assigned to perform background checks. Mikie gave the young woman a list of names to check out. At the top of the list was Genevieve Rice, but she also wanted to know about the other counselors, the director and his assistant, the therapist, and Paul's parents.

"If anyone has medical training, you can focus on them, but don't stop looking into the others."

The young cop looked wary. "This is a long list."

"You're lucky it isn't longer. I left the campers off it. I might add them back later."

"When do you—"

"Yesterday," Mikie snapped. "Ask for help if you need it, but don't bitch about it."

She was annoyed, but mostly with herself. Now fourteen hours had elapsed, maybe more. She hadn't established a headquarters or closed off a crime scene. Whoever had given Paul Anderson insulin had had plenty of time to clean up after himself. Or herself.

Mikie remembered standing in the lodge. What she sensed there was intangible, unprovable, and worthless to the DA: the will to murder, which lingered like a wisp of smoke, the stink of it in the air. She had been at countless crime scenes, and she could count on one hand the times she hadn't sensed where death had been violently dealt. *Damn!* She had known better.

"Ma'am? Do you want me to do anything with the 911 call?"

"Like what? We know who called." Mikie was already moving toward the door.

"The other one, I mean. The one from two days before? About the fire?"

Mikie turned. "What fire?"

The newbie paled slightly. "There was a 911 call to Heritage Camp on the twenty-third? I thought you knew. A fire in one of the cabins."

"Who responded?"

"Dispatch sent a fire truck, and I guess the marshal went over there later. No injuries, just damage to some boxes. But there were some questions, um, some question about how it started, from what I gather? Detective Wu got the information, so I assumed...sorry, ma'am," she finished breathlessly.

"Thank you," Mikie said. She had to unclench her teeth to say the words, but she meant it. She walked straight to Wu's office, but he wasn't there. His desk was covered in papers. There didn't appear to be a particular order to the chaos, but she didn't have to look very long to find the 911 call—it sat on top of his inbox. The call had come from a cell phone on July twenty-third. Some papers in a cabin caught fire, but the fire was extinguished by the time the pump truck arrived. There had only been minor structural damage, and camp staff had put the fire out with an extinguisher kept on site. The source of ignition was thought to be a cigarette.

The staff member who put out the fire was Paul Anderson.

Mikie intercepted Wu in the parking lot.

"Hey," he said. "I'm just back from interviewing the nurse. I think we might have enough now to—"

"How is it I didn't know about the fire?" she said.

He cocked his head slightly. "The fire," he repeated.

"At Heritage Camp? Big and green, you might recall it? It's our crime scene?"

"There was a fire? When?"

"Jesus Christ," she said. "It was sitting in your inbox."

"What? Jeannie knows not to put things in my inbox. She always calls my cell."

"Jeannie's in Maui. She got married on Saturday."

"Shit," he said. "I haven't seen my desk in two days. I've been working this case is why. Don't look at me like that, Mikie. You know I'm not a slacker."

Do I? Mikie thought. *What do I know?* The known world was sliding around under her feet. The facts rolling in were improbable, even impossible. Paul Anderson put out a fire at Heritage Camp two days before he died. Somebody put insulin into his well-developed quadriceps. And then there was her dad. Nothing seemed like a stretch at this point.

"This type of thing can't happen," she said, then handed him the paper describing the 911 call. He read it at once. "You better speak to the desk and make sure they know how to get information to you."

"And to you," he said. "You might ask yourself why nobody called you."

"What's that supposed to mean?"

"Just that if I missed the message, so did you."

"We're talking about your inbox, Wu. You're my secondary," she said. "You're supposed to stay on top of the details."

"I am. Do you want to hear what I learned at camp? I collected a few more details that might interest you." He looked annoyed but, thankfully, not rattled.

"Tell me on the way to the Anderson house," she said.

"So we're not arresting the nurse?"

"We don't have enough."

"Detectives?" The newbie stood in the doorway. "This came through on the fax just now?"

"And you were about to put it in my inbox," Wu said. He and Mikie made eye contact and, to her surprise, she couldn't help but smile. She looked away. "Listen, Officer..."

"Jones. Tiffany."

"Do me a favor, Tiffany Jones," Wu said, "and pretend I don't have an inbox. Call me for every little thing."

"Yeah, um, that kind of goes without saying?" she said. "I was hoping to hand it to you directly, but if you weren't here I totally would have called."

"Well then, totally thanks." He looked at the fax and his smirk vanished.

"What?" Mikie asked.

He handed her the paper. Someone had printed the following message in block letters:

CHECK PAUL ANDERSON'S PHONE PHOTOS. BLACKMAIL.

"Where did it come from?"

"The fax number's printed across the top?" Tiffany said. "I looked it up and it's from that camp in Sandy? Heritage."

Chapter 17

July 26, 2:00 p.m.

"I can't think," Hal said. He slammed his laptop shut with some vehemence and shoved his balled-up fists into his eyes, displacing the sunglasses so they covered his forehead.

Police were everywhere. They had arrived suddenly and in great numbers. From his tree, Isaac spotted first one police car, then another, then a van. Each vehicle was flanked by clouds of red dust. The cops drove a lot faster than the parents.

Isaac and Hal sat alone in their cabin. Nathan was busy helping the kids who were going home—gathering their possessions, scrambling to collect phone numbers, email addresses, and the art they'd made. The scene in the parking lot was catastrophic, as though an earthquake had hit or Mt. Hood had erupted. Parents couldn't get their kids away fast enough, but the police held them up, speaking to every camper, however briefly, before they left. The parents waited impatiently, hovering, their eyes darting around as though camp had turned dangerous overnight, with killers poised in the woods. It was stupid. Nathan said they were overprotective, and Isaac supposed this proved his point. He'd texted his own parents already, telling them emphatically that he wanted to stay put.

The peanut butter cup wrapper was somewhere in the cabin. Hal said it was better if Isaac didn't know where, exactly. Isaac expected an officer to knock on their door at any moment and every noise startled him, but Hal seemed oblivious to any risk.

"Kids are freaking out," Isaac said. His own pulse was pounding in his throat. "We're withholding evidence, aren't we?"

"What? No. Well, maybe. But having a peanut butter cup is hardly a crime."

"No, but...what do you think about the insulin thing? Wasn't that a strange thing for the cop to ask about?"

"Isaac," Hal said. "This line of thinking is unproductive. Sophie did not kill Paul."

"But..."

"She is incapable."

"But you don't know everything," Isaac said miserably.

Hal stopped rubbing his eyes and let his sunglasses fall back into place. "What facts, exactly, am I missing?" Isaac opened his mouth and closed it again. "Isaac. Tell me what you know."

"I don't think that would be a very good idea. I mean, for Sophie."

"It is absolutely in Sophie's best interest for me to have access to all possible information."

"But what if it makes her seem kind of suspicious?"

"You think your information implicates Sophie?" Isaac nodded, miserably. "It doesn't."

"You don't know what it is yet," Isaac protested.

"The specific facts are irrelevant, insofar as Sophie could be implicated. I know she didn't do anything to harm Paul. As to what did happen—well, I'm at a bit of an impasse. But I promise my knowledge will not harm Sophie. In fact, it will do quite the opposite."

Isaac took a deep breath. He told Hal about the other night, starting with seeing the video of Sophie on Paul's phone and ending with Sophie storming off from the dock. He related the story in as much detail as he could remember.

"Then I didn't feel well, and I went to the infirmary."

"That's everything?"

"No! Then last night Sophie, like, freaked out. While you were sitting at the dock. She said it was all her fault, and then she fainted."

Hal looked at him sharply. Then he shook his head. "It's no good," he said. "You'll have to get me some Adderall."

"What? Why?"

"Non sequitur, sorry. My brain isn't working. I can't help Sophie if my brain doesn't work. Hence, the Adderall request."

"Do you have a prescription?"

"Of course not. Stuff's dangerous."

"Well, how am I supposed to get it then?" Isaac asked, exasperated.

"The black market, obviously."

"But—I wouldn't even know where to start."

"I do."

"And it's massively against the rules!"

"Rules," Hal said, scowling. "Arbitrary guidelines. They're for sheep. I'm no sheep."

"Then why don't you get it yourself?"

"I'm too well known. You, Isaac, are a tabula rasa. No one knows what you're capable of. And, frankly, you haven't been here long enough for anyone to really worry about you. Plus, it might be interesting for you. Like Sophie said— don't be so expletive careful all the time."

Chapter 18

July 26, 2:50 p.m.

The Andersons lived in a newish development south of Portland proper, where most of the homes looked empty and featured "For Sale" signs punched into the dirt. Each lot was oversized, and most of the lawns hadn't been filled in with sod yet. Big as the lots were, the houses generally filled most of the space. Mikie found them unattractive and bloated, with attached two- and three-car garages and no front porches.

"You know this was farmland until maybe fifteen years ago? Kind of a shame," she said to Wu as they turned into the Andersons' driveway. They'd gone with the Tudor model. A big English flower garden would have been perfect, but plain grass went right up to the house. There were three cars in the driveway and a plastic tricycle on the lawn.

"Looks like they have guests," Wu said.

Before they arrived at the front door, it opened and a little tow-headed girl in a diaper came running out. She had the top-heavy gait of a toddler, and when she saw the detectives she stopped, backed up, and almost fell over. A woman right behind her steadied the girl with both hands. "Mama! Dada! Mama! Dada!" the girl said.

"Can I help you? This isn't a great time," the woman said, looking harassed. She was petite with light-blond hair and pale eyes, which she kept trained on the little girl.

"Sorry," Mikie said. "I know it's a bad time. We're with the Oregon State Police. We need to speak with the Andersons about Paul."

"You do know what happened, right?"

"Yes. We just have some follow-up questions."

"But why...when it was an accident...oh, never mind. Come on in," she said, touching her hair. "Maya, come on now, honey." She gently steered the little girl back inside.

"Muck! Muck!"

"You want some milk, okay." Then she turned to Mikie and Wu. "Who do you want to speak with? I'm Paul's Aunt Linda, Terry's sister."

"Both parents, please. It doesn't matter who's first." After Linda and the toddler disappeared at the end of the hall, Mikie and Wu looked around. The hallway wall was crowded with family photos. They saw Paul as a little kid in an astronaut costume, no doubt for Halloween. Several family portraits featured Paul flanked by his parents, and these illustrated the march of time: Paul was a small child, then a preteen, then a young teenager with braces, then a good-looking lanky kid of about eighteen, taller than his pregnant, blond mother. A photo printed on canvas showed him as a young man in a baseball uniform. His skin was clear and he looked calm and confident—a kid with a future.

Mikie noticed a large framed painting that seemed to be the work of a child. It was multicolored and abstract, done with a thick brush. "Do you like it?" a man said behind her. Mikie settled her expression and turned around.

"It's interesting. Did Paul do it?"

"An elephant painted it," the man said. He was about fifty, Mikie figured. He smiled politely, but he looked exhausted. His hair was brown with plenty of gray in it, and there were deep purple shadows under his eyes. "No, really," he went on, as if she'd argued the point. "We saw it done. It was at an elephant sanctuary. In Thailand, where we adopted Paul. We stayed an extra week and visited some temples and things. They teach the elephants to paint and play polo. I assume they're treated better than wherever they were rescued from, but the trainers still use sticks and hooks." When he stopped talking, his face looked haunted. Maybe he knew it, because he started talking again. "Paul was afraid of the elephants. But he got brave as the day went on. By the end, he was feeding them bananas. We were going to go back when Maya was a little older. He wanted to show her the elephants."

"Mr. Anderson," Mikie said as gently as she could, "we've gotten some new information that we need to check into. Could we look around Paul's room?"

"What new information?"

"I can't say more than that, I'm sorry. It may be nothing. An anonymous suggestion. They usually turn out to be groundless, but we're obligated to rule these things out."

"What could there possibly be to rule out?" Mr. Anderson said. His voice was low, but there was a tension in it. Maybe anger, or grief. Or both. "My son is dead. He had an allergy and some idiot broke the rules and it killed him." His voice cracked on the final words, and he visibly tried to control himself, breathing heavily.

"The circumstances are strange enough that we're checking into every possible angle. Including the possibility that it was something other than an accident."

"Not an accident? What does that mean? Is this about that damned life insurance policy? Is that what this is?"

Mikie felt, rather than saw, Wu glance at her. "Let's sit and talk a minute, please, Mr. Anderson. I don't know anything about life insurance. Sounds like Detective Wu and I need to be filled in."

He looked at her furiously for a moment. Then he deflated, suddenly becoming old and tired again. "It's not like things could get any worse." He led them down the hall, through the expansive kitchen, and out the back door. "We can sit on the deck. I'm trying to let my wife sleep. She's not doing very well. I hope you won't feel the need to bother her."

Mikie didn't respond. She hoped the same thing, but with the way things were going, she doubted it would work out that way. Mr. Anderson thought things couldn't get worse, but he was wrong. She had seen it happen. A lot of times she made it happen.

They sat in comfortable padded deck chairs at a round glass table. Mr. Anderson didn't bother to put up the umbrella. "Can you say more about the life insurance?" Mikie asked. "Was Paul insured?"

"He insisted on getting it this past winter."

"Did he say why?"

"We were taking out loans for college—he got into Reed. He was worried about how much we were borrowing. He thought if anything happened to him...I told him not to be silly, nothing was going to happen to him, and if it did, his student loans would be the last thing on our minds."

"That seems unusually considerate for a kid his age."

"That's Paul for you," Mr. Anderson said, his face brightening momentarily. "He's always been that way. When Maya came along he was so thrilled to be her big brother. Of course, he could practically be her father."

"She's adorable," Mikie said.

"What is the age difference, anyway?" Wu asked, sounding merely curious.

"Eighteen years. What a surprise she was. My wife thought it was menopause. But thank God it wasn't. If it weren't for Maya..." He rubbed his forehead with one hand. He seemed to notice the sun at last and patted his shirt pocket, looking for sunglasses.

"Was it because of Maya that he wanted to get insurance?" Mikie asked.

"That's exactly what he said. I wouldn't have anything to do with it. He went himself and took out a policy. He was over eighteen, so he didn't need us to do it."

"But why did he think he needed it?" Wu asked, glancing quickly at Mikie. She nodded imperceptibly. "I have teenagers myself. They never think anything can happen to them."

"He said...he was concerned because of his allergy. There have been a few high-profile stories in the news—" Mr. Anderson stopped. Mikie saw him struggle to compose himself. She felt the pain that rolled off of him in waves. *Stop it*, she told herself.

"I understand," she said, almost brusquely. "He wanted you and Maya to be protected in case it happened to him."

Mr. Anderson nodded. The pallor was gone, and his face was scarlet with the effort to control the tears that poured down. He gasped. "I'm sorry," he said. Then he gave in and sobbed. It was Wu who reached out and put a hand on his shoulder.

In the end, Mr. Anderson let them into Paul's room upstairs. "Be as quiet as you can," he said. "And please, leave things the way they are. My wife needs the room to stay the way it is right now." Surprisingly, Paul's mother was curled up on his bed, wrapped in a childish quilt. Mikie nodded her understanding, and Mr. Anderson withdrew.

They looked around. The room was pretty empty. His cabin at Heritage Camp had contained more personal effects. Of course, he was going off to college, so he may have been partially moved out. The furniture consisted of a double bed, a desk and chair, and a digital piano on a stand. Everything but the keyboard was white—walls, furniture, lamp, and a small fluffy rug beside the bed. A large cardboard box sat beside the closet, overflowing with towels and bedding, and a smaller box beside it was filled with books. A poster of Ichiro Suzuki in a Mariners uniform was the only decor on the wall. The closet contained winter coats, a baseball bag, and a couple of aluminum bats resting in the corner. There were worn baseball mitts on the closet shelf. But there was no computer.

Mikie slid the desk drawers open one at a time and found paper clips and mechanical pencils, along with a few pennies and nickels. Wu checked the closet, running his hands over the walls and the undersides of the shelves. There were drawers under the bed, and they opened them as quietly as they could, finding only winter clothes and musical scores. They withdrew to the hallway.

"Surely he had a computer," Mikie said.

"No laptop at camp, either. We looked."

"Let's ask his dad."

Mr. Anderson didn't know where it was, either. "He had a MacBook," he said. "It went to camp with him. I haven't seen it."

"They didn't return it with his things?"

"I just said that."

A woman entered the kitchen on silent feet. "I know where it is," she said. Her voice was rusty, as though unused for years; that, or she had screamed and sobbed herself hoarse. She was small, like her sister, and wrapped in a bulky hooded sweatshirt. Her hair was a brunette tangle falling past her shoulders. In the family photos, she wore a neat updo, smiled, and stood straight, looking nothing like the woman who stood before them.

"Honey, I've got this," Mr. Anderson said, moving to her. "You woke her up," he said without heat.

"Mrs. Anderson?" The woman looked at Mikie as though she was seeing her through a sheet of ice. Mikie stepped a bit closer. Maybe the woman was taking sedatives. "I'm so sorry to bother you. I know you're exhausted."

"You aren't from camp," Mrs. Anderson said. "The school?"

"The police. I'm Sergeant O'Malley. You can call me Mikie. And this is Detective Jim Wu."

"Why...police?"

"They say it's just routine," Mr. Anderson said. "You can go back and lie down, love."

"In just one moment, please," Mikie said quickly. "You have Paul's laptop, Mrs. Anderson?"

"It's in the baby's room. I don't...know why. He needs it. For college." Mr. Anderson wrapped an arm around his wife's shoulders and avoided the detectives' eyes.

"Lie down now. Come on."

"Thirsty," she whispered as he led her to the stairs.

"I'll bring you something."

Mikie and Wu looked at each other as the Andersons went upstairs. Wu's eyes said, *He knew where that laptop was.* Her look replied, *Yes, he did.*

Mikie's phone rang. "It's Colin," she said to Wu, then answered. "We're putting you on speaker in a sec." She and Wu stepped outside to speak without Mr. Anderson overhearing.

"You asked me about the phone," Colin said without preamble.

"Did you get into it?"

"Sorry, have we met? I'm Colin, IT ninja."

"Of course. Apologies."

"It wasn't that hard to get into, actually. It was fingerprint protected, so I had to go to the morgue. That's always fun."

Dark humor. It was familiar to her from hospital work—one of the things that hadn't changed in her new career. "What did you find?"

"A lot had been deleted. But I retrieved some interesting stuff. I was able to get into emails, and it looks like he might have been selling term papers. Or maybe keeping track for someone else. I won't go into details unless you want 'em."

"Term papers? That doesn't seem like a big deal," Wu said. "They're all over the internet."

"That's not all. He'd received and deleted a couple of photos and videos...some boys, some girls, mostly looking pretty young."

"Porn?" Wu asked.

Awaiting the answer, Mikie thought about how much she hated this part. Paul Anderson, by all reports, had been a nice kid—a camp counselor, a good son, a caring older brother. Now she had to learn his secrets, destroy that comforting image, and cause unimaginable pain to his family. And it probably wouldn't be worth it—except that they might have his killer.

"Not porn. They show people using drugs. Smoking what looks like weed, mostly. Some of them are kids smoking out of pipes, a few are snorting something. It looks like they didn't know they were being photographed or filmed. He'd deleted almost all of them."

"Can you tell when he deleted them?"

"About eight months ago. One arrived the day before yesterday. Guess he didn't have a chance to delete that one."

"Where did they come from?"

"A few different numbers. I already checked the last one and it's a burner phone, disposable."

"Fantastic," she said. "Don't go anywhere."

"Hold up! I have dinner plans!"

"We'll bring you a pizza."

They opened the door to the house to find Mr. Anderson walking heavily down the stairs to the foyer. There was a white laptop under his arm and a resigned expression on his pale face.

Chapter 19

July 26, 3:00 p.m.

Every thirty seconds, Isaac changed his mind. He wasn't going to help Hal chase an Adderall buzz. It was ridiculously risky, and he had nothing to gain. Half a minute later he decided, *screw it*, he was no sheep, either. He wanted to know what had really happened, and he somehow believed Hal would figure it out.

To make things worse, what Hal called the "black market" required an incredibly elaborate system. Isaac suggested he could just complain about feeling sick and hang out in the infirmary. With Genevieve so distracted, and Sophie right next door, it would surely be possible to snitch a couple of pills out of the cabinet where she kept the prescription drugs. Genevieve usually left the key in the lock. Better still, Hal could do it! But no. Hal said that would be stupid, that Isaac was sure to get caught, that the black market was a storied institution of Heritage Camp, and that, furthermore, he was curious to identify the involved parties.

Isaac noticed that he was starting to think the way Hal talked. It was disturbing.

Following Hal's instructions, he wrote "ISO 3–5 DOSES ADD" in block letters on a piece of paper and tacked it up in the third stall of the boys' bathroom. No one was around other than Max, who was waiting impatiently outside. He was filling in as Isaac's "buddy" while Hal did whatever it was he did on his computer. "Genotypes and phenotypes and some mid-level hacking," he called it.

Isaac's heart was going like a bongo when he rejoined Max and walked to the arts-and-crafts building with him. The day was growing overcast and he shivered when the wind blew, but the cabin was warm and filled with campers. It smelled like glue. A couple of large windows let in the light.

A tiny woman stood over one of the many round wooden tables where campers sat among a riot of decorations—feathers and sequins and other doodads. Her hair was in a loose knot and her shoulders drooped. When she turned to greet him, Isaac was startled to recognize Tanya Miller. She was beautiful as always, with smooth, light-brown skin, high and delicate cheekbones, and full lips. But her eyes were dead and she looked ragged. She must have been ill, just like he'd thought.

It would be nice to say "I told you so" to Hal, but he didn't take any pleasure in the thought of Tanya being sick. Even if he was right about her and Paul. On second thought, could it be that grief, not illness, was making her look so terrible? Before he could follow that train of thought anywhere, she spoke.

"We're making masks today," she said. "You can decorate yours any way you want. The way you see yourself, or the way you want the world to see you."

How did he want the world to see him? That was easy: he wanted to be an ordinary boy; to stand out as little as possible. Other campers were gluing feathers and sequins, drawing flags and musical instruments, birds and peace signs. Isaac made his as simple as possible. He colored it in light brown, added a small smile—no, that was too *Mona Lisa*. He erased it and made his mouth neutral. That was all. Isaac, the tabula rasa. Impostor, sneak, Adderall thief: all was hidden. He was so absorbed in the activity that the hour passed quickly.

On the way to the next activity, he glanced at his watch. "Dude," he said to Max. "I gotta use the bathroom again."

"What? You just drained that weasel!"

"You don't have to wait for me. Just go."

Isaac ducked back into the stall. He didn't really expect it to have worked. But his paper was gone, replaced by a scrawled phone number in pencil and the words "ERASE THIS." He memorized the number, spit on a piece of toilet paper, and erased it. As he jogged back to the cabin, trying to look casual, he spotted movement through the trees. Police officers in uniform were walking in the forest, looking at the ground, and moving leaves and rocks aside. A surge of anxiety—no, terror—started somewhere in his solar plexus and surged throughout his body. By the time he reached the cabin, his fingers were trembling. Hal sat impassively at his laptop.

"This is insane," Isaac hissed. "There are cops everywhere."

"Did you get a response? A phone number? A meeting place?" He didn't take his eyes off the screen.

"We got a phone number. Hal? Are you hearing me? There are police in the woods. Searching for something. And what you want me to do is illegal."

"You've already done something illegal. Give me the number." He dialed and let it ring. "No answer, no voicemail."

"Good," Isaac said. "Because I don't want to—"

"During AGT tonight, take a picture of your exact location and send it to the number."

Isaac threw his hands in the air. "I am not doing this! I don't even want these pills, you do! And I'm not participating in some illegal transaction with a bunch of police around!"

"Oh. My apologies, Isaac. I thought you wanted to figure out what happened to Paul."

"No. What I want to do is help Sophie."

"This is how we do that."

"But—"

"Relax. In any case I never planned to send you to do the pickup."

"No?" Isaac felt a mixture of relief and, oddly, disappointment. "Well, good."

"No. You're far too nervous. Your job will be well suited, I believe—climb a tree, somewhere close by. Right after you send the text. Go as far from the campfire as you can. I'll be in position to observe you, but you won't see me."

"Judo magic?"

"If you like."

Isaac was about to leave, but he stopped. He had to know. "Hal?"

"Yes, Isaac."

"You said you know Sophie didn't do it."

"Right."

"But why are you so sure?"

"Sophie is a pacifist. That means she wouldn't hurt anyone."

"I know what a pacifist is," Isaac said, annoyed. "I want to know how you know...how you can be so sure."

Hal closed his laptop. "Fine. If you must know, then I'll tell you. But first," he said, "it should be fairly obvious that you can't divulge what I tell you to anyone else."

"Okay," Isaac said. He sat down on the bed across from Hal. He hoped the twins wouldn't come back too soon.

"Second...a question. Have you ever wanted to kill a person?"

Isaac could think of a few possibilities. The bullies who had made life unbearable popped into his mind. Even at the worst moments, though, the person he'd mostly wanted to kill wasn't them. Working with Michelle, he'd managed to get past even that. Still, he thought he could understand the feeling.

"Sort of," he said. "Almost."

"Did you make a plan? Did you think it would work? Did you take any steps to make it happen?"

"No," Isaac admitted.

"Well, I did," Hal said. "It would have worked. I know it. And I wanted to do it."

Isaac's throat felt dry. Even though he couldn't see Hal's eyes, the conversation felt so intimate, he had to look away.

"Who?" he asked.

"It was the person the state calls my 'father.' He has plenty of money and it appears from the outside that he gave me the best of everything. Private school, judo lessons. But he is not a good person. He doesn't deserve to live. And my life, along with my foster brothers' and sisters' lives, would have been unquestionably better with him dead. It seemed quite simple to me. Please don't ask me any questions about him because I never want to talk about him again. Never."

Hal was crazy. Isaac didn't know how this had escaped him before. "Well, why didn't you do it?" *Please say you couldn't go through with it*, he thought.

"Simple." Hal smiled. "Sophie said no. She was quite persuasive. She said that if I killed him, he would never have the chance to realize what he'd been doing was so wrong. And that he should have the chance to learn that, and to feel the pain from doing wrong. That didn't really persuade me, but she also said that if I killed someone, I would be a murderer. She said it would change me forever, that she loved me the way I was, and that she wouldn't feel the same way about me if I were a murderer. That's how strongly she feels about killing."

"What...what was the plan?"

"It doesn't matter. It was terribly clever. Now go away for a little while, Isaac, if you don't mind. I'm finally making some progress."

Isaac started to leave, then realized he couldn't go without understanding one more thing. "Hal? You and Sophie...you said she loved you?"

"Friends, Isaac," Hal said firmly. "Friends since forever. Romantic love is not in my bailiwick, nor does Sophie feel that way about me. Fortunately."

"Oh, okay."

"Now go away."

Isaac smiled, feeling lighter inside. "Going."

Chapter 20

July 26, 4:00 p.m.

"I'll warn you right now, these are pretty depressing if you have kids," said Colin. They were in his extremely neat office, going through Paul Anderson's MacBook. Colin was overweight and ginger-haired, and the only mess was a pyramid of empty Diet Coke cans on his desk. He had a lot of electronics on his shelves. Mikie recalled him having thick glasses, but he must have gotten contacts or had laser surgery on his eyes, which now looked strangely prominent—bright blue and intelligent.

"Just let me catch one of my daughters doing this," Wu muttered, looking through the printouts.

"How old would you say they are?" Mikie asked Colin.

"I'd say between thirteen and twenty. Hard to be sure. There's some overlap with the phone, like this video. This is the one that was left on the phone." He pointed and clicked, then turned the MacBook so they could see the screen. They saw a striking Asian girl with pink streaks in her hair snorting a crushed-up pill, then falling backward, looking inert, her shirt pulled up over her abdomen. Wu pointed. "Freeze that image. Look at that. Look at her right leg." Mikie leaned in. It was easy to miss, considering the distracting foreground, but Wu was right: there was something odd about the way her right leg looked.

"Colin, can you pull that up and zoom in?"

Once the image was enlarged, they could see a gap just below the kneecap. Colin went to his own computer and tapped some more keys, then said, "If you enhance the color saturation, you can tell that the leg below the knee is a different color. Look. It might look like a perfect match, but there's a lot more white and yellow in the lower part of the leg."

"So it's what, a prosthesis?" Mikie asked.

"I'd say so. If the gap wasn't there, it might just be a matter of sun exposure to the upper and lower legs—although usually the lower leg will be darker, not lighter. But in this case it's almost certainly a prosthesis, unless the image was jimmied in some way."

Mikie asked, "Can you tell when this one was taken?"

"Uploaded...last November. Of course, that doesn't mean it was taken then."

"What else did you find?"

"Photos of Anderson. Looks like he was out of it. Someone snapped him with a bottle of pills in his hand, sent it to him." They leaned in and stared at a photo of the handsome boy, apparently asleep, a white plastic cup of pills tucked into his curled-up hand.

"Weird," said Wu. "That doesn't prove anything, except one of his friends is an asshole."

"What are those pills supposed to be?" Mikie asked.

"The PDR identified them as twenty milligrams of OxyContin, extended release. They fetch about twenty bucks apiece on the street."

"*PDR* being...?" Wu asked.

"*Physicians' Desk Reference*. We have the electronic version. It's not foolproof, but it's pretty good, and the pills look real. Plus, when you zoom in you can see the ID numbers."

"Colin, can you use facial recognition to tell who these kids are?" Mikie asked.

He waggled his head. "Yes and no. If there are enough tagged pictures of them on the internet, then generally, yes. But the tech isn't perfect. You tend to catch siblings and other close family members in the same net, and it's especially hard with kids because their faces change. With these kids it's going to be more difficult because, honestly, facial recognition is racist."

"What do you mean?" Mikie asked.

"The tech is only as good as the people who build it. In the US that means all kinds of biases are built into the system. In short, it sucks at identifying anyone who isn't white. It'll probably get better with more time and inputs."

"Figures," Wu scoffed.

Mikie asked, "What else did you find on the drive?"

"I already told you about the term papers. There are copies of papers together with hyperlinks to sites on the internet where the same paper's for sale. That's about everything of interest on there."

"What about internet searches?" Mikie asked.

"He spent most of his time in incognito mode, which makes it more difficult to follow him everywhere he went. We can do it, but it will take time. The stuff he did under his own sign-in was mostly about traveling in Thailand. Looks like he read about Buddhism a few times in the past couple months. And he followed the Mariners, poor kid."

Wu was paging through the printouts again.

"Do you recognize anyone else, Wu?" Mikie asked.

"No. I don't see that girl in any others, either."

"Thanks, Colin," Mikie said. "You've given us plenty for now. See what you can do with identifying some of those faces."

She and Wu walked down the hall to Mikie's desk. "We need to go through all the photos to see if there's anything to this blackmail thing," she said.

"I suppose that would be my job."

"No, I'll do it," she said. "I'm going to learn more about the life insurance, so I might have some downtime. I'd better get moving, though, the office probably closes at five."

"What about Dad?"

Mikie knew what he was asking. Whether they needed to look at the other computers in the Anderson home. "I think it can wait."

He looked frustrated. "While we're waiting, Dad might wipe the hard drives."

"Colin can retrieve most anything."

"Not if he throws it in Lake Oswego."

"Nothing leads to Dad," Mikie said, "and he has an alibi. Bible study, remember? I can't see it. Even if motive is there, he didn't have the opportunity unless he snuck into camp and somehow fed his only son—"

"Adopted son," Wu interrupted.

"You think that makes a difference?"

Wu shrugged. "Maybe the attachment isn't as strong. Now that they have a kid of their own and a big tuition bill at Reed."

Mikie squirmed a bit. There was a sour taste in her mouth. "I'm not sure it works that way. But you know what? You can ask the therapist, Tanya something—Miller. Why don't you head back over there? Find out who might've used the fax at 10:07 a.m."

"Yes, ma'am."

"Keep your eye out for the girl from the phone."

He smiled. "One leg, pink hair. That shouldn't be too difficult."

It took one call to Tiffany Jones—who was turning out to be quite efficient despite her tendency to end every sentence in a question mark—to learn that Genevieve Rice, formerly Genevieve Hartog, had no criminal record and an active nursing license in good standing; that Ty Janssen had been expelled from the honors program at Lewis & Clark College in his fourth year for reasons unknown but non-academic; and that Katie Matthews, the assistant director, had a single MIP (minor in possession of alcohol) from her senior year in high school two years ago, which was officially expunged from her record so that your average background checker wouldn't be able to find it.

Otherwise, the counselors were an unusually clean-living group. That or their families were connected, important types whose children could act out without official consequences.

That rarely works out in the long run, Mikie thought. She recalled the weekend over a decade ago when her oldest brother, Christopher, borrowed their uncle's red Miata without permission and went joy-riding with a sixteen-year-old girl. They had a minor accident, colliding with a cement barrier in a parking lot, which unfortunately caused the girl to break her bottle of Corona and lacerate her upper lip. Mikie's father was furious enough to leave Christopher in jail for the weekend, although he sleeplessly paced the house the whole time, worrying about him. Every dollar her brother earned for about two years went to paying off the fines and fees he had incurred. And, as her father had predicted, it didn't hurt him any. He was a urologist now, living in California, and so stuffy and square it was impossible to imagine his youthful hijinks.

It took longer—three phone calls—to find the insurance agent who had sold a policy to Paul Anderson, since Mr. Anderson didn't know who Paul had worked with. Mikie went to the office without an appointment, hoping to catch the agent before he left for the day.

The receptionist insisted that Mr. Dollarhyde was in an important meeting and balked at interrupting him. Mikie decided she'd give him fifteen minutes before barging in. She sat with her back to the wall, opened Paul Anderson's laptop, and scrolled through the pictures. No one looked familiar, although some of the girls—they were mostly girls—could have been campers, she supposed. One of them might have been Katie Matthews, but it was hard to tell because the photos were of poor quality. Many of them had been taken from videos, had time stamps in the corner, and were severely pixelated. What they had in common was the expression on the kids' faces after using. They looked blissed out, blank; like all their worries were erased. She could almost, though not quite, see the appeal.

After only five or six minutes, the inner door opened and two men walked out, laughing and clapping each other on the shoulder over some joke. One of them, pale and balding with an old-school comb-over, spotted Mikie over the other man's shoulder. She flipped her badge open without a word. It was satisfying to watch the heartiness drop several notches.

"You've made a great decision. Now keep in touch!" he said to the other man. He practically shoved the client out the door before turning to Mikie. "Well! Portland's finest! How can I serve? Let's head back to my office." Once they were inside he said, "Listen, I have told you people, I understand the requirements. I won't miss another appointment. There is no reason to harass me at the office."

Mikie had chosen not to alert him in advance to the reason for her visit. Apparently, the receptionist hadn't clued him in either. She said, "You recall Paul Anderson."

She watched his expression morph from annoyed to worried to puzzled to relieved. Then it reverted back to puzzled. "What about him?"

"You sold him life insurance." The last trace of concern vanished from the man's face. She supposed he was lousy at poker. "Look, whatever your issue with the law may be, I'm just here for information. Paul Anderson died late last night."

"He did?" He looked surprised. "But he was just a kid! What happened? Was it peanuts?"

"What makes you ask that?"

"Paul Anderson—allergic to peanuts, right? That's why he wanted the policy, he said."

"You remember a lot about him," Mikie commented.

"I don't get many his age interested in life insurance. What a shame. What happened?"

"We're still investigating. The family hasn't contacted you, I gather?"

"No, I had no idea."

"What kind of policy did he get?"

Dollarhyde got up and crossed to a file cabinet. "I can show you."

"It's not in the computer?"

"I keep a hard copy with signatures. Anderson...it was a standard term policy. I tried to talk him into whole life, which would have protected him for decades, and served as a nice investment too. It's really a better deal. Your money earns interest over time, and your premiums stay the same as you age and your risk profile increases. Here it is. Two hundred thousand dollars."

Mikie looked the papers over. There were dozens of boxes, all checked NO. No heart disease, no kidney problems, no hospitalizations. Under family history he had written, "Adopted, no info available." She recognized his spiky handwriting from his health forms.

"Why did he choose this policy?" she asked.

"Well, I assume he wanted to keep the premiums low."

"Don't assume, please. Just tell me what he said, exactly, as near as you can remember."

He gazed at her with interest. He was a big man, but he had little eyes and a delicate, pointy nose that reminded her of a fox. "I'm really shocked," he said. "When I sold him the policy, I had no idea...was there foul play of some kind? It wasn't suicide, I hope?"

She tried to sound patient. "What did he say?"

"Let's see. He wanted a nice policy that would cover his student loans and leave something for his family. I believe he had a younger sibling—yes, a sister."

"But why did he say he needed life insurance?"

"Because of the allergy. He was planning to travel and he was afraid he might have a reaction."

"Where was he going?"

"Someplace where they cook with peanuts a lot, he said. India? Thailand? Yes, that's it, I think. We discussed Thailand. Beautiful beaches. Beautiful people too."

"He was from there," she said.

"Yes, I think I knew that."

"Did he say when he was going? Or how long he'd be gone?"

"Not that I remember. He didn't say much at all, really. I only asked because I was curious why such a young man wanted life insurance. It makes perfect sense, of course: everyone should have it. But most young folks don't see it that way. Let me see...he wanted to make sure if he died overseas, the policy would pay for him to be shipped home. Didn't want to stick his parents with the bill for that—it can be very expensive. But his policy was enough for that and more." He was comfortable now, on familiar territory.

"Thank you, Mr. Dollarhyde. One more thing. When I told you he'd died, you asked if it was foul play or suicide. Why did you say that?"

"No real reason. It does happen. My first guess was actually peanuts, you might recall. Suicide is unique, though, because it's excluded. Insurance companies don't pay anything out for suicide."

"Did Paul Anderson know that?"

"It was in the policy he signed. He's supposed to have read it before signing. We didn't talk about it at any length."

Mikie was leaving when Dollarhyde spoke again. "Detective? I almost forgot...and maybe you know this already...but young Mr. Anderson asked me to recommend a lawyer too. He wanted to make out a will."

Chapter 21

July 26, 6:00 p.m.

Whatever Hal had done to the internet must have worked, because he dove back into cyberspace and showed no signs of surfacing, even for dinner.

"It's fish sticks," Isaac said. "Brain food." But his "buddy" merely grunted, so Isaac left him there and sat instead with Nathan and the twins. Their table was sadly empty. Amazingly, the twins were subdued. It took a minute for Isaac to realize they were playing on their phones between bites. This was a violation of the strictest Heritage Camp rule: no electronics at meals. But Nathan didn't seem to notice, or if he did, he didn't care.

"You okay?" Isaac asked.

"I guess." His gaze kept roaming around the room.

"Who are you looking for?"

"No one. Where's Hal?"

"Not hungry. He's working on his project thingy—says he has no energy left over to digest food."

"That kid!" Nathan smiled. "Unique, no?"

"He's all right," Isaac said. He felt protective, which was stupid. Hal could protect himself.

"Oh, I know he is. I'm not saying anything bad."

"He's a dick," Max said to his plate. His long hair hid his face.

"Freak," David agreed through a mouthful of tater tots.

Isaac looked at a point just past their heads. "Uh-oh, I think he just heard you."

Panic flashed across the twins' faces until they looked long enough to be satisfied he was kidding. Isaac grinned until he saw the policeman come through the door. He'd just gotten used to the uniformed officers roving around; they didn't seem as scary now, but this one was in regular clothes, so he must be one of the detectives. Maybe they called the detectives in when it was time to make an arrest. Or when they found something.

Like a peanut butter cup wrapper.

He turned back to his food. The fish sticks suddenly looked heavy and unappealing, but he was still hungry. Thirsty too. He got up to get himself more apple juice and mandarin oranges, keeping the cop in his peripheral vision the whole time. The man's gait was graceful; he seemed to glide around the room.

Was he looking for someone in particular? Isaac didn't see Sophie, or her mother. Trying to think the way Hal thought, he realized Tanya Miller was also absent. Ty was here, though. He'd spotted the detective and wheeled over for a word. After a couple of minutes the two of them left the main lodge and went down the hall. Isaac took a long sip of his apple juice and tried to decide what to do. He could feel his heartbeat speeding up again. In a couple of hours, he'd be at AGT. (Who would perform? That could be ugly.) And then he'd be involved in a drug deal. The whole point of coming to camp was to be inconspicuously himself—a normal teenage boy. And here he was. Every decision he made, it seemed, put him more at risk. *What the hell?* he thought. *Don't be so fucking careful all the time.*

He wanted to know what had happened to Paul—as long as it wasn't what he feared. But what if it was? He realized he wanted to know that too. If Sophie had done it, he might be able to understand—he might be the only one who would. Even if it was partly his fault.

He strolled to the bin, put his plastic cup in it, and walked casually over to the door that led to the hallway. He hoped no one was looking and dared a quick glance over his shoulder. Zero eyes were trained on him. He kept walking, experiencing a feeling of unreality. It was only a few hours ago that he'd been here with Hal. The office door was closed. He opened the broom closet door—it was just as silent as before—and stepped inside.

Chapter 22

July 26, 6:30 p.m.

Mr. Anderson didn't look surprised to see Mikie at the door again. He looked at her expectantly, asking nothing. She waited a few seconds, then realized he was dreading the moment she opened her mouth and made their family secret, their family shame, official.

"You knew I'd be back," she said.

"You have the laptop," he said and shrugged. His face seemed to have collapsed even further since the morning, like punched-down bread dough.

"I'm sorry. I know it's painful. But do you know if your son used drugs?"

He rubbed his forehead with one hand; he made no move to invite her in.

Finally he said, "He struggled...no one's perfect."

"Of course not," she said, carefully. "So you know he used?"

"He did at one time, but he'd stopped."

"Do you know what kind?"

"Hydrocodone. OxyContin. My son has—had—an addiction." He continued to stare at a point off in the distance. "But he was a good person. He was in therapy, taking medication for the anxiety that probably made him use drugs in the first place. He was doing well."

"I'll need the therapist's name," Mikie said.

He met her gaze at last. He looked honestly bewildered. "Why? What can she tell you?"

"I don't know yet. Did anyone else know about the drug use?"

"Only the people who absolutely had to know."

"Do you know if your son was strictly using drugs? Do you think he sold them, too?"

His skin flushed deeply. "My son wasn't a drug dealer. He was a straight A student with a problem. You have some nerve, asking me that."

"Mr. Anderson. I'm obligated to ask difficult questions, and you're obligated to tell me the truth. That's the situation we find ourselves in." He didn't say anything. He was breathing hard. "Could he have sold drugs to someone else?"

"Why?" he asked. "Why are you asking me that? Did someone kill my Paul?"

"That's what I want to know." Gently she said, "I'm sure you know how a parent would feel about the person who sold drugs to their child—or if they thought the person did, even if it wasn't true."

"I don't know. I don't believe it, but I don't know."

"Who would know, then?"

"Just Paul. Paul and God. And maybe his therapist. Tanya Miller is her name. You'll find her at camp. Please leave now," he said. The pain on his face was unmistakable. A wall. She was on the other side. "Don't come back until you have an answer."

"I just have one more question. Was Paul planning to go to Thailand?"

He shook his head.

"Would you have known it, if he was?"

His eyes were the flattest, the most miserable, she had ever seen. When he spoke, it was with obvious effort. "College. He was going to college."

She nodded and turned to go. "If you think of anything else, please call me."

"Detective? Do you believe in hell?"

It was unprofessional to answer, but she nodded. She knew why he'd asked.

Mikie called the main number at the station, hoping to catch Tiffany Jones, although it was late enough that she might have left for the day. She was pleased when Jones answered the phone.

"Sergeant! I have some information for you. Do you want it now, or when you come in?"

"I don't know if I'll make it back in tonight. Better tell me now."

"Okay, um, you asked me to find out if Paul Anderson went to the hospital before? After the fire on the twenty-third? He did. But he went to Adventist, not to Emanuel. He was treated for burns and released."

A break, Mikie thought. She used to work there. Her best friend from nursing school, Rachel, still worked in the Adventist ER as far as she knew. She'd go by there tonight, she decided. "Good work. What else?"

"I called a lot of lawyers? All of them in his hometown, and a few of the bigger names in Portland? Not everyone answered, but so far it looks like he didn't make a will with any of them. Maybe he did one on his own? I know a lot of people do that online or use Quicken."

"Okay." This was disappointing, but not a surprise.

"And there's more if you're ready."

"Go on."

"So I looked into Ty Janssen? He was expelled from university here, right? But he got into a pre-med program in the Philippines." She pronounced it *Philip-pines*, like the tree. "The University of Cebu. You do a year of pre-med and then you're admitted automatically to their medical school. Or some people go to a different med school. Anyway, it turns out he was kicked out of there too."

"Do you know why?"

"It's the middle of the night there—thirteen hours ahead? The person I spoke to didn't have the authority to say. But I'll try in a couple of hours. They should open by nine."

"Aren't you about ready to go home?"

"Oh no. I can stay. This is a really interesting case?"

Someone was going to have to do something about all these question marks. But not tonight. "Tiffany. Officer Jones. Thank you for all this, and for staying late. Call me as soon as you learn anything."

She called Wu but got his voicemail. "Before you leave camp, talk to Tanya Miller. She was Paul Anderson's therapist. And call me. I want to hear what you learned about the fax, so leave a message if I don't answer."

Chapter 23

July 26, 6:30 p.m.

The closet door didn't squeak, which was a lucky thing because Ty and the cop were right next door in the office. Isaac could hear them perfectly, even the sound of the detective's chair scraping the floor. A sneeze would be disastrous. *So don't sneeze*, he told himself.

Isaac barely breathed. He felt strangely calm. Maybe he was so scared that his whole terror-awareness system had overheated and shut down. That seemed like the only possible explanation for the way his hands didn't shake and his heart didn't bang away on his sternum as he leaned over and peered through the pencil-sized hole in the wall of the broom closet.

"—glad you're here, Officer."

"Detective, actually, but you can call me Jim."

"Jim, that's nice of you."

"What makes you so glad to see me, Ty?"

"I found something you need to see," Ty said grimly. "I don't know what it means." He opened his desk drawer and handed over a scrap of paper. Wu leaned forward and looked at it without touching it.

"Where'd you find it?"

"It was in his clarinet case. Down by the campfire."

"You recognize the writing?"

"It's Paul's."

"Where's the rest of it?" The cop was taking something out of his pocket—a plastic glove. He took hold of the paper.

"I have no idea. That's all that was in there."

"And the clarinet?"

"No idea. It wasn't there."

"Where's the clarinet case now?"

"Gosh, I don't know. It was here—not in the office, but in the lodge. Detective—I mean, Jim—what do you think this means? I can't believe—I mean, it's totally awful to think—have you seen something like this before?"

"Like what, Ty?"

"Well, suicide is what comes to my mind. Although I can hardly believe it."

"Why'd you look in the case?" The cop was suddenly abrupt. But when Ty spoke, he sounded thoughtful, not shaken.

"I don't know, really. It was just there. The clarinet, it was like a part of him. I wanted to see it, touch it. I had the idea...it was still warm from his hands. I know that sounds silly. More likely it was from the fire anyway."

"What fire?"

"We had a campfire. Paul played for the campers while they ate s'mores and all that."

"I hear there was another fire. No one mentioned it when we were here."

"God, that's right! I forgot all about that. Our therapist apparently left a cigarette burning in her office. It was a small fire, not much damage, but the fire department came. We probably won't be hiring Tanya Miller again—smoking is expressly forbidden in the employee contract. But Paul used the fire extinguisher and put it out before the truck arrived." His voice thickened. "That was so typical of him." He pressed the heels of his hands to his eyes.

"Was he hurt?" If the cop was sympathetic, it didn't show in his voice.

"What, in the fire? I don't think so."

"Did he go to the hospital?"

"If he went anywhere he wasn't gone long enough for me to notice. But I really doubt it. If he'd needed to go, I would have been more than happy to take him. I guess you can ask his campers. They'd be more likely to notice if he disappeared for a while."

The cop took their names, writing them in a little notebook. Isaac heard his own name and felt a chill run down his spine, but it quickly passed.

"We got a fax from Heritage Camp today. I need to know who sent it," the cop said.

"From here? Are you—no, of course you're sure. The fax machine is right behind you." When the cop looked around, Isaac couldn't help it—he stepped back and collided painfully with the shelf behind him, the corner of which punched him in the back of the thigh. He stifled a yelp and rubbed the spot. He'd have a bruise later. And now he'd missed part of the conversation.

"—could have sent it, really. What time was it sent?"

"Why don't you tell me where the staff was throughout the day, instead."

"Sure! Here's the basic schedule." He found a sheet of paper, made some notes on it with a pencil, and pushed it across the desk. "We're a little off-kilter today with everything going on. But Katie can help. She's the detail-oriented one around here."

"Ty, you mentioned suicide. First we've heard the word." The cop's voice was warm and slow again.

"Only because of the note! I didn't say I thought he did it."

"Were you close?"

"Close as two people can be—no, not like that. We were fostered together. We were literally like brothers, years ago in Thailand."

"And you kept in touch all this time?"

"No, it was a coincidence we met again. Well, not a total coincidence. Several of us came to the States through a church program around the same time. Paul first, me a year or so later. Our parents went to the same church. We ended up at the same high school, though we were a couple grades apart; I graduated when he was a sophomore."

"That right? You're older but he got here first?"

"I came with...certain challenges." His smile was wry, and his gesture encompassed the wheelchair, the stunted legs, the pockmarks on his round face. "Paul was like the holy grail, a cute, healthy baby boy." He sighed. "I can't believe he's gone. It's so stupid."

"Work with me for a minute here. Do you believe Paul would have killed himself?"

"No. Although— but no. It was years ago, and...I'm pretty sure he was over it. Kid had everything going for him. He was stoked about college."

"What was years ago?" Wu asked. Ty compressed his lips, seeming reluctant to go on.

"Don't leave me hanging," Wu pressed.

"It's just—he had really bad anxiety, okay? Not like ordinary shyness, I mean he was phobic around new people. School was torture for a while. But don't make too much of that. He was doing great the past year."

"Did he discuss suicide with you?"

"We did talk about it in kind of a general way. How to do it, if things got too bad. But they weren't bad, not anymore."

"How to do it? Suicide? What did he say? Would he have eaten a peanut or something?" *No*, Isaac thought. *No way.*

"No. He thought anaphylaxis would be horrible. I can't believe he would have done it that way."

"What would he have done if things got too bad?"

"He said it would be easiest to give himself a shot of insulin."

Chapter 24

July 26, 7:20 p.m.

Mikie parked in the Adventist employee lot and walked over to the emergency department. For a moment she felt like a time traveler—she could have been arriving for the night shift. Her locker might even still hold her sneakers and clogs and a couple of granola bars from ten years ago.

She didn't miss that life. It was every bit as exhausting as police work, although it seemed like people had liked her better. But rarely, as a nurse, had she experienced the profound satisfaction that she now got from solving a case. In both roles, though, she'd been lied to. *No, I don't smoke. I can't be pregnant; I've never had sex. I never even saw that bag of meth, it's not mine!* She was good at spotting liars, but learning how often that skill was required had put a real dent in her faith in humanity.

She was pleased to see Rachel White at the intake desk, leaning over the harried-looking receptionist and hijacking her mouse. She looked the same as ever—colorful scrubs, blond hair braided back tightly off her face, maybe a couple of new wrinkles by her eyes as she squinted at the screen in front of her.

"Hi, Rachel."

"Mikie! Holy Hannah, it's been a while. You okay? You're not here as a patient?"

"It's work. I'm fine. You real busy?"

"Nah. Moon's not full and it ain't Saturday night. What do you need? Are you here to buy me dinner?"

"If you have time, that'd be great."

"Let me just check."

"Before you do, can you look at a chart from the day before yesterday? Or bring it with you?"

"I'll bring my tablet. Who are you interested in? Quietly, now." She glanced around, but the hallway was empty.

Mikie wrote "Paul Anderson" on a page from her notebook and showed Rachel.

"Oh! I don't need to look him up. I took care of him. I'm on days now—seniority. I'm just covering for a friend tonight."

They went to the cafeteria. She and Rachel picked sandwiches from the cooler and carried them to a small table in the corner. Mikie tried to pay, but Rachel waved her off and used her employee badge.

"Cute young guy," Rachel said when they were seated. "Slight accent. I thought it was a little odd for a guy named Anderson."

"Wait, accent? Was it this guy?" Mikie showed her Anderson's picture in the camp directory, and Rachel studied it.

"Sure looks like him."

"Are you sure?"

"Pretty sure. Why?"

"How badly was he hurt?"

Rachel spoke in a low voice. Mikie had found that cops were a lot less concerned with confidentiality than nurses.

"Fairly serious burns on both hands, but not over a large area. He needed dressings and follow-up. No plastics consult or anything. It was palms and wrists mostly."

This made no sense.

"Big dressings?"

"Not huge, but you'd notice them, being on the hands. Like mittens. Oh yeah, he also got a tetanus booster, since he didn't know when the last one was. If he'd been a kid he'd have been in the system, but he was nineteen, I think."

"No one considered admitting him?"

"Heck, no. Just second degree. If he'd had decent first aid, he wouldn't have needed to come in at all."

"Thanks. This is—well, very interesting."

"Happy to help. He's a cutie," she added with a smile.

Mikie sighed. "Unfortunately," she said, "he seems to be dead."

Rachel clapped a hand to her mouth. "What? What happened? It wasn't the burns? It couldn't be!"

"No." Mikie hesitated for just a moment, then summarized the situation for Rachel. "The weird part—one of the weird parts—is that he had an autopsy, and there were no burns on his hands. I'm not just going by the report, I was there. Also, I don't think our victim had an accent, although I didn't ask."

"Weird!" Rachel was shaking her head. "Is he a twin?"

"Good question. He's adopted." For a split second she was tempted to share with Rachel what she'd recently learned about her dad. But now wasn't the time.

"That's how this would work on TV." She looked at the photo again. "I don't know. This sure looks like him."

"Can I ask you something else?"

"Make it snappy, I only have three more minutes." She took a big bite of her sandwich.

"Can a person tamper with an EpiPen?"

"You mean so it doesn't work?"

"That, or so it dispenses insulin instead of epi."

Rachel frowned, chewing. She shook her head and swallowed. "Is that what happened to your victim?"

"It seems like it."

"Would that even be enough insulin? I mean to kill a person? They're pretty small." She pulled out her phone, brought up a calculator, and did the math. "I think they only dispense, like, point three mils. I don't think that would be enough."

"Maybe enough to tip someone over, though. If they were already having anaphylaxis?" Mikie felt a bit silly about her theory, saying it out loud to another nurse, but there was no arguing with the pathology report.

"Thirty units of something fast-acting, probably NovoLog...I mean, that would give a person a pretty good headache, but it wouldn't really hurt them. Unless it was U500."

"What's that?"

"Hardly anybody uses it, but it's five hundred units per mil. If you need, like, hundreds of units per day, it's less volume to inject, so it makes life a little easier."

"So what'd you say, point three mils? That would fit a hundred and fifty units, right?" Mikie asked.

"Yep. And that's a different story. But I can't imagine how you'd get into it."

Mikie took out her new EpiPen and handed it over.

"I've seen them before," Rachel said. "I've even given one a few times, but I never thought about how to sabotage one."

"Me neither."

Rachel's phone made a noise. "Shoot, I've gotta run. Let me know how it turns out, Mikie. And keep in touch!" She gave a quick hug. "You'll figure it out. You were always the smartest cookie in the jar. Smart enough to get out of this job!"

Mikie fiddled with the EpiPen and hoped Rachel was right.

Chapter 25

July 26, 7:30 p.m.

Jim Wu left the main lodge, relieved to be out in the open air. He hadn't shaken the director; in fact, the young man in the wheelchair had rattled him. Wu didn't trust Ty Janssen. The note bothered him. It was too convenient, too well timed. *I know this will be hard for you to understand.* It could have meant anything. Mr. Camp Director was awfully quick to hint at suicide, and he'd known about the insulin. How would he know that if he weren't involved? But would he have said it aloud if he were responsible? Would he have looked so calm? He didn't sweat; he didn't flush or get pale. They'd sat close enough to see each other's pupils, and Ty's were steady. He seemed legitimately surprised about the fax—and curious, though he hadn't asked outright what it said.

Wu always felt a little awkward around people in wheelchairs. He didn't want to stare, but he didn't know where to look. It was something left over from his ballet training, where strength and grace were an obsession, almost a fetish. He knew it was a prejudice; knew he had to conceal it.

But he had the sense that Ty could tell.

He listened to his voicemail, heard the message from Mikie telling him to talk to the therapist. He decided there was no harm in talking to the nurse first, though. He went by the infirmary where a line of rambunctious kids stretched out the door. A couple of kids were swinging on the porch glider. The nurse was at her desk, dispensing pills and paper cups of water.

Wu said, "You look busy."

"Evening meds," she said without looking up. "And I have one throwing up in the back, so I hope you don't need me right this second."

"Will I find you here later?"

"I'm not going anywhere."

He didn't feel entirely comfortable walking away—she was the one who'd wielded the EpiPen. He wanted to arrest her, never mind what Mikie and the DA said. But he had his orders, and it was probably for the better that they didn't include hauling off the camp nurse in front of a bunch of gawking kids. Then he spied the picture on her desk.

He recognized the girl from the video on Paul Anderson's phone—the one where she was snorting drugs. Of course, in this picture she looked quite different: standing with her mother and a man, presumably her father, in front of Haystack Rock at the beach. In the photo, Genevieve was smiling, her face happy and relaxed. She looked quite different from the harried woman in front of him. He couldn't tell from the picture whether this girl had a prosthetic leg, and her hair didn't have any pink streaks, but he was pretty sure it was her.

"Cute kid," he said. She frowned, deepening the creases at the corners of her mouth, and he realized that could have been the wrong choice of words. "I have a couple teenagers at home myself. They grow up so fast. She must be your daughter."

"Mm-hmm. Elliot, you forgot your vitamin," she called to a camper who looked about eight years old. He bounced back and opened his mouth for what looked like some sort of gummy candy.

"What's her name again? Your daughter? She goes to camp, yeah?"

"Sophie," she said. "Officer, this isn't the best time. Could we—"

"Sure. I'll catch you later." He went on with a bit of extra spring in his step. Motives always cheered him up. If he was right about Sophie, surely Mikie would agree they could arrest her mother.

He walked back to his car to call Mikie, but she didn't answer. As he listened to the phone ring, a flash of orange caught his eye: a fluttering piece of paper on the windshield. *Trash*, he thought, and he got out of the car to pick it off and throw it away. But then he noticed two things simultaneously. One, it was a Reese's Peanut Butter Cup wrapper, and two, it was tucked under the windshield wiper as though it had been placed there deliberately. He pulled his hand back, glad he hadn't touched it. He put on a glove, pulled a Ziploc bag from the glove box, and slipped the wrapper in the bag, then put it in his pocket. He looked around, wondering who had put the wrapper there, whether they were watching him now, and what it meant. *Probably some kid*, he thought. But why? *Well, why do kids do anything?* he wondered.

He thought about the pictures Colin had showed them earlier and decided to make a quick call. His older daughter, April, didn't answer. The phone rang a couple of times and an unbidden image came to him of her glancing at the screen, seeing his name, and ignoring him. She would be texting her boyfriend, of course. That or playing something online. He made a mental note to check later that her password hadn't changed. This was one of the many things he and his wife—ex-wife, he tried out, although they weren't yet divorced—didn't agree on. "Kids need their privacy," Joy said. He'd laughed, imagining what his own parents would have thought about that when he was fourteen. He wasn't even allowed to use the phone without a stated reason. Laughing had been a mistake, one of many he had made where Joy was concerned.

"Hi April," he said to his daughter's voicemail. "I'm leaving you an old-school voicemail you probably won't listen to. I'll see you tonight, I hope. I love you. Be nice to your sister." Before he had the chance to hang up, the phone vibrated in his hand. It was Shiloh.

"Hi Daddy!"

"Hi, baby girl. What's happening?"

"April says to tell you..." Her little voice was breathless and he grinned.

"Take a breath, baby girl." He could hear voices in the background, sounding impatient.

"April says she's playing Dragon City so her eggs are hatching and she can't answer and don't get mad at her. And also can we get pizza." He heard April in the background, correcting her. "I mean, Uncle Henry's getting us pizza later."

"That sounds good." The girls were staying at his parents' place with him this week; his brother must have stopped by.

"When are you going to be home?"

"I don't know yet, Shi. I might have to work late. But you can save me a slice of pizza, okay?"

"Okay. Bye Daddy."

His next stop was Tanya Miller's cabin. Mikie's message said she'd been the victim's therapist. It was interesting no one had mentioned that before. But then, Anderson's death had seemed like an accident. He followed Ty's directions and found the small A-frame in the woods, surrounded by Douglas firs. He ignored the "Do Not Disturb" sign and knocked. *Homicide detectives didn't hesitate to disturb*, he thought—*or impose, inconvenience, or annoy.* There were times this aspect of the job gave him pleasure, but he did hope he wasn't interrupting a session with a troubled youngster.

It took a long couple of minutes for her to come to the door. When she did, he inhaled sharply—and, he hoped, silently.

She was gorgeous. Tiny. Southeast Asian, he thought. She was dressed in a black T-shirt and white linen trousers, wearing no makeup, her hair pulled back and clipped up loosely. She waited for him to speak, but his mouth was dry. Ridiculous. Instead, he showed her his badge.

"Yes?" she said. "How can I help?"

"I have some questions for you about Paul Anderson. The young man who died."

"Yes. I know who he is." Her face was still and calm, no trace of anxiety, guilt, or fear. But there was something. "Can it wait about five minutes? I'm in a session, but we're just wrapping up."

"That's fine. I'll wait out here if that's okay."

"Please be comfortable." She gestured to the chairs on the porch.

He waited gladly. He needed a minute, truthfully. The air smelled great—the cabin was red cedar, and the trees all around were the fragrant type. Beneath those smells were the comforting odors of wet leaves and the lake. A hint of smoke. He walked around the cabin looking for scorched areas, but there weren't any that he could see.

This wasn't a bad gig, he guessed. Spend the summer in the woods, help kids with their issues, read by the fire at night. It probably didn't pay much. Camps didn't employ cops, anyway. Although considering this case, maybe they should.

He would have to be careful with this woman—Tanya Miller. Her name had not prepared him; he had expected someone completely different. Social workers, in his experience, were either young and hippie-idealistic or middle-aged and disillusioned. Almost always, they were white. He closed his eyes, slowed his heart rate, and prepared his face to intimidate, interrogate, and detect. Not to woo and be wooed. *Or Wu and be Wu'd,* he thought. Then he shook his head. *Get ahold of yourself, you idiot.*

After five or six minutes, she opened the door and joined him on the porch, sitting beside him on a battered Adirondack chair. He wondered where her "session" was. Still inside? Or was it fictitious? "I don't know your name," she said.

"Jim Wu. I work with Sergeant O'Malley. She's spoken with you on the phone, but we haven't been able to arrange an interview in person."

"But why interview me? Not that I mind. I'm happy to help if I can."

She had a slight accent that was familiar. He once knew a Thai woman, a fellow dancer, who had worked hard to get rid of her accent, but no matter what she did she couldn't say "Kleenex"; it came out "Klee-neck." He had a sudden, irrational desire to hear Tanya Miller say "Kleenex."

"I actually can't say much about it," he said. There had been no need for that *actually*, he knew. "We're looking into the Anderson boy's death."

"Of course." She waited. He couldn't think of a single question.

"Did you know the victim?" he asked stupidly.

"I know all the counselors, at least a little. I also saw Paul as a client. Perhaps you already know that."

"What was your impression of him?"

She widened her eyes as though surprised by the question. "You mean a general impression? He was a fine person. Patient with the children. Everyone liked him. I liked him. Is that what you mean?"

"That, yes, and how did he seem to you in the days before he died, or even on the day itself? What was his mood?"

She shrugged at "mood," as though shaking off a chill. "He was healthy and seemed happy. I'm not sure what you mean. And then..." She paused for a moment to choose her words. "I'm not sure how much I need to tell you. My sessions are confidential. Death doesn't necessarily change that."

"Sure it does. Nothing you can tell me can possibly hurt him now."

"It cannot help him either," she said immediately. "And of course it could hurt. Not him, but his reputation, his family members, his friends."

"In this case?"

"I can't say, I'm afraid. But if you want to ask me questions, I'll answer them if I can. If I can't, I'll tell you so."

"Easiest thing in the world to get a warrant, you know," he said.

She didn't miss a beat. "But you do not have one now."

He couldn't argue with that. "Okay. Did he seem depressed?"

"No."

"Was he depressed before? In the past?"

"Not depressed exactly, no."

"What, then?"

"He had anxiety issues, primarily."

"Would it shock you if it turned out Anderson committed suicide?"

"It cannot shock me because it isn't true."

"How can you know that?"

"The whole idea is ridiculous. He died of an allergic reaction, in front of dozens of people." Her cheeks were slightly pink.

Wu said, "I'm not saying it's what happened, or even that it's likely. But some information has come up that means we have to at least rule it out."

"What information?"

"Sorry. Can't say," Wu said.

"How many suicides have you known?" she asked suddenly. "Any?"

"That's not really—"

"Because I have known several, more than a few, through my work. And in every case, there were warning signs. Always. There were none here." She stood up, suddenly looking agitated. "You asked if I knew Paul. I knew him very well. He was not depressed. He was not in despair. He had plans for his future and he was very excited about them."

"Okay," Wu said. "If everything was so wonderful, why did he need the Paxil?"

It took her a moment to respond. "That's not relevant."

"Actually, it is. Besides, we know he had social anxiety disorder."

"Then you know the reason for the Paxil and you didn't need to ask me."

She was angry now, no question. Strangely enough, he felt more comfortable. He was still attracted to her, but other than that it was becoming a typical witness interview. "Okay. Fair point. Sit down. I didn't mean to be sneaky. I just need information and I'm trying all my usual tricks to get it."

She sat. "I understand. But I think this is a waste of time."

"You're probably right. Still. Can you tell me about social anxiety?" he said. "You can just talk in general terms, not necessarily about Anderson. I mean, is it really a thing? Is being shy serious enough to need drugs?"

Tanya bristled again at the question. "Not always. There is a spectrum. It's not just shyness. Some clients do better on medication."

"Did Paul?"

"I thought we were talking in general. But yes, he was doing great," she conceded. "We discussed stopping the medication but decided the timing wasn't right."

"Could he have gone off it without telling you? Had a downward spiral?"

"No."

"You sound very sure of that."

"I suppose you could check the bottle, but I'm sure he would have let me know."

"Okay. What about conflicts with campers? Or other counselors? Any relationship you know of that maybe went south?"

She sighed. "Now you're really wasting your time, Officer. And mine."

"Detective, actually, but Jim is fine."

"Okay. There is no way Paul killed himself. Jim."

"Why didn't you change cabins?" he asked suddenly. He saw the question catch her off balance, as it was intended to. "After the fire?"

"There was no damage," she said. "Just some papers burned, luckily."

"You don't look like a smoker."

She shrugged. "I don't smoke much. Just sometimes."

"Wacky weed? Or regular coffin nails?"

"I beg your pardon?"

"Regular smokes, or what?"

"Regular cigarettes," she said.

"What kind?"

"Whatever kind is on sale."

He hid his smile. Smokers were fanatically brand-loyal; she was lying. This cheered him for some reason. Maybe just the fact that he could spot it. "One last thing. Do you recognize this handwriting?" He watched her closely as she scanned the faxed note and analyzed the message. Maybe he imagined it, but it seemed she blanched a bit. "No," she said.

"Any thoughts about what it might mean?"

"I—can't say."

"Can't say or don't know?" She shook her head. "We know he had a lot of pictures on his phone. Pictures that might have caused serious trouble. Who wrote the note?"

"I don't know. Is this all?"

"Almost. This next question might be a little weird, but my boss wanted me to ask. Do adoptive parents love their kids, do you think? I mean really love them?"

She stared at him. "I can't imagine why you're asking me this question."

"Because you're an expert. Surely you've worked with lots of families. Let's say a family adopts a child. Then a few years later they have one of their own. Would they be likely to treat them both the same? Or would they maybe prefer their child?"

"The question doesn't make sense. Adoptive parents also consider their children 'theirs.' Every family is different. But yes, generally, adoptive parents love their kids."

It wasn't his imagination now: Tanya Miller was holding herself together with effort. If her indignation flagged, she'd collapse, he thought. He handed her his card with the usual talk about calling if she thought of anything. She practically fled inside.

Interesting woman, he thought. He hadn't met a woman that interesting in a long time, let alone had a reason to give one his number. It was a shame she might be a suspect.

Chapter 26

July 26, 7:45 p.m.

By the time Isaac let himself out of the broom closet and slipped out of the lodge, the sun was just starting to go down, and dark gray clouds were scudding across the sky. It was risky to follow the cop; insane to spy on him. Instead of trailing around after him, Isaac decided to climb a tree that offered a reasonably decent view of the whole camp. But he didn't want to be out in the open, so he chose one near Tanya's place. From there, he saw the man leave the infirmary, disappear from view for several minutes, then approach Walden cabin, where apparently he intended to speak with Tanya.

He couldn't hear everything—just the suggestive cadence and song of an argument—but he knew when Tanya got upset, because her voice rose like the dust and reached the trees.

He decided to alert Hal to the situation. Holding onto the tree with his elbows, he sent a brief text: "Cop at Tanya's. I'm in tree." His head was crowded with questions and empty of answers: What did the cop mean about suicide? Why did insulin keep coming up? Did it mean they suspected Sophie? Most of all, he wanted to know what the note in Paul's clarinet case said—and the fax. It seemed probable that Katie had sent it, but why? What did it say? Hal would have thought of a way to get a look at the pieces of paper the two men had shown one another, but Isaac could only wonder and worry.

When the therapist's door closed, the cop walked away, looking slightly dazed for some reason. He shook it off, though, and headed back toward the clinic. Then Isaac's phone made a noise: *ba-loop.*

Damn! The man looked up. Isaac froze, but it didn't do any good.

"See a lot from up there, do you?" the policeman called. "Bet you know everything that goes on around here."

"Not really," Isaac said. He had to clear his throat.

"Come down here, young lady. You and me are gonna talk awhile."

Isaac gasped, but he didn't see any alternative. He shimmied down. The cop said, "What's your name?"

"Isaac." He cleared his throat again. "Whitson."

"Oh. Ah, sorry about the young lady thing."

"It's okay. I didn't see anything, though."

"Why were you up there?"

"I like trees." Isaac toed the ground and felt his face grow hot.

"I like 'em too. But humans don't live in trees anymore, and generally they don't climb them without a reason. I'm a detective, Isaac, and when I ask you a question, you need to speak the truth. You understand that? How old are you?"

"Fif—I mean sixteen."

"Sixteen?" He sounded surprised. Isaac knew he was on the small side but found this reaction discouraging. "Why'd you say fifteen?"

"I just turned sixteen. I forgot for a second."

"You forgot? When's your birthday?"

"May thirtieth."

"What year?"

Isaac had already observed the abrupt, startling way this cop asked questions. If he hadn't, he would have been petrified. As it was, he felt only mildly terrified. "Um, do I need a lawyer?"

"A lawyer? Why? To tell you when you were born?"

"No, I—"

"What's your name again? Isaac Whitson, is it?" He nodded. "Isaac, did you set any fires recently?"

"No, never—"

"You kill anybody?"

"What? No—"

"Then, my arboreal friend, you are not under arrest. You are not a suspect in any crime. I have no plans to charge you with anything. Is that clear?"

"Yes, uh, Officer."

"Detective. That's Detective Jim Wu you're speaking to. Now. Who put this wrapper on my car?" He pulled from his pocket a Ziploc bag containing an orange wrapper. Isaac gaped, finding himself without the power of speech. "Well? You had a pretty good view from up there. You got nothing for me, Isaac? Got something against the po-po?"

"The what? No, I don't think—"

"You know what obstruction of justice is? Hindering an investigation?"

Isaac swallowed. "Just from TV."

"Did you know Paul Anderson?"

"He was my counselor."

"Good guy?"

Before Isaac could respond, he noticed Hal walking up behind the cop. *Thank God*, thought Isaac. He was happier to see Hal—those dorky shades and the "Free Geek" T-shirt—than he had ever been to see anyone.

"The best," Hal said. Detective Wu turned around.

"And who might you be?"

"My name is Hal Shaw, sir. I was well acquainted with Paul, whereas Isaac here is just a newbie. No pejorative intended, of course, Isaac. Detective, you might address your questions to me, if you like."

The cop looked amused. "So you did bring your lawyer," he said to Isaac. "Now, Hal, I want to know who put this candy wrapper on my windshield. Isaac here was in the lookout perch."

"Oh, was he in a tree again? That is a risky habit, Isaac, but fortuitous if you saw anything. Did you?" Isaac shook his head. "A shame."

Detective Wu said, "I suppose you didn't see anything either."

"No, I was in my cabin working on a software program for school."

"That's diligent of you. Especially in July."

"How kind of you to say so," Hal said. He sounded utterly sincere.

"Why are you wearing those groovy shades, anyway? Kind of flashy, aren't they? You have some vision problem, or what?"

"In a way. My vision is unusually acute. The light tends to hurt my eyes."

"Well, tell me about Paul Anderson. I could use some extra acuity," the cop said.

"Certainly. He was an extraordinary person. Kind, intelligent, and shy. Quite a talented musician; he played the clarinet. What else would you like to know?"

"That's his cabin, yeah?" He pointed at the right A-frame.

"Yes, and ours as well. Would you like to have a look?"

"Why not? You can give me the guided tour."

They walked in and looked around, which didn't take long. The twins were elsewhere, but the air was redolent with their sharp, musky smell. They must have cleared out recently. The detective didn't look at either boy as he asked, "So who was Paul's girlfriend?"

One eyebrow peeked out above Hal's sunglasses. "Fraternization isn't allowed at camp, sir."

"Fraternization isn't—oh, come on. Boys and girls together for the whole summer? In the moonlight, by the lake? Who's gonna be able to put a stop to that?"

"Six weeks, actually. And Paul generally followed the rules. I don't think he was with anyone."

"What about that cute girl with the prosthetic leg and the pink-and-black hair...what's her name again?"

"Sophie?" Isaac said and regretted it instantly. His face grew warm. The cop looked at him with barely concealed triumph. Hal didn't say anything.

"Thanks, boys," the cop said. He shook hands with Hal and high-fived Isaac, who returned a weak slap. *Police 1, Isaac 0*, he thought. "I gotta motor, but I sure appreciate the information."

When he was gone—Isaac made sure he was really gone, counting twelve steps, thirteen, fourteen, fifteen—Isaac said, "I'm sorry. I shouldn't have—he tricked me into saying the name."

"As I've reiterated, Sophie, being innocent, should not be in danger. One hopes the authorities will realize that."

"But what if they don't? Nathan saw her kissing Paul right before—before it happened. And there's some connection with insulin, and she's the only here who uses it! And then there's the video, and I told her who had it."

"Relax, Isaac. We're not going to permit anything to happen to Sophie."

"We're not?"

"Of course not. Besides, the detective is about to be redirected." He looked smug.

"What does that mean?"

"The peanut butter cup wrapper isn't the only item to make an appearance on his windshield. Just before I walked over here, I saw Ty leave him a fat manila envelope."

Chapter 27

July 26, 8:30 p.m.

Wu answered on the fourth ring, just as Mikie was about to give up. "I found out about the insurance," she said without preamble. "It's true: Paul went on his own. He even asked for a referral to a lawyer so he could make a will, but I haven't found it." There was a pause. "Wu?"

"I'm looking at it," Wu said.

"What? How is that possible?"

"Somebody left it on my car."

"You left your car unlocked?"

"Of course not. It was on my windshield."

"Well who left it?"

"I don't know. Security camera must be down." This was a joke. The previous week, the superintendent had announced his intention to put cameras on all the cars. Like there was money for that.

"Does it look legit?" Mikie asked.

"I think so. It's a DIY job. Looks like he used a program."

"Who witnessed it?"

"Interesting," he said. "Ty Janssen. Katherine Matthews—"

"That's our Katie, the assistant director."

"—and a Nora O'Brien. That's the notary public, actually. It's dated June sixth. Just, what? Eight weeks ago."

"That's the day after he bought the insurance," Mikie said. "I want a look at that will. Let's meet up. I have something too." She told him about her hospital visit and the fact that a nurse identified the photo of Paul Anderson as her burn patient from two days ago. "He wasn't a twin, as far as his parents know. I can't get ahold of anyone from the agency at this hour. I called Grace to make sure I'm not losing my marbles, and she says categorically no burns and no tetanus shot in the arm. The nurse says her patient had both. Billing agrees, by the way—they charged Anderson's insurance."

"This is getting weird," Wu said.

"Any idea who left it on your car?"

"I know who didn't leave it: Tanya Miller and these two kids I just met. Otherwise, it could be anybody. Janssen, maybe. And that's not all. I found a peanut butter cup wrapper on the windshield a little earlier. Someone stuck it under the wiper blade."

"A peanut butter cup?"

"Just the wrapper."

They were silent for a moment. Mikie asked, "Who's still there from the department?"

"Me and two uniforms—Jason and that new guy."

"Leave them there and I'll meet you close by. What's that restaurant next door? Beside the U-pick berry place?"

"The Tippy Canoe? All right. What about Nursey?"

"Stop calling her that, she has a name. She's not likely to go anywhere, but you can have one of the unis keep an eye on her," Mikie conceded.

"Maybe that's not enough. Didn't you listen to my voicemail? Turns out the girl in the picture is her daughter, name of Sophie."

"Is she at camp?"

"She is. I also met a kid who has it bad for her. Why don't I talk to her first?"

"No," Mikie said. "I want to be there. I'll come to camp; we can eat afterward."

"How close are you?"

"Fifteen minutes."

She took Interstate 84 to Corbett and turned off at exit 18, back to the winding road along the Sandy River. She ignored a call from her dad, suppressing a feeling of guilt and then a spurt of irritation. He should understand that she was on a case and didn't have time for conversation—especially one that might involve complicated feelings, regrets, explanations.

When she arrived, she found Wu in his car. He got out and waited as she parked. When she emerged, he said, "Janssen says he didn't leave the will. He was doing paperwork in the office the whole time."

"You believe him?"

"I don't know. Miss Katie confirms it, says they were filling out forms together. I asked her about Sophie. She's staying in the nurse's cabin right now, next to the infirmary. Timing's perfect. Nurs—I mean, Ms. Rice just went to the lodge, so we can talk to the girl alone."

Mikie hesitated before nodding in agreement. The girl might be a suspect, in which case they'd need parental consent and a responsible adult present for the interview; but at the moment, she was just a possible witness. They were within their rights to talk to her without her mother, although there was no doubt Genevieve wouldn't like it.

They entered through the outside door to the infirmary but found the inside door locked. When Wu knocked, the door to the left creaked open. A pretty teenager with streaks of color in her black hair peeked out. Her eyes were a startling shade of blue.

"Do you need my mom? She'll be right back." Her voice was hoarse, as though she'd been sleeping. She yawned, covering her mouth.

"Are you Sophie?" Wu asked.

Her expression was wary. "Mm-hmm."

"You missed dinner, Sophie."

"I guess."

"I'm Detective Wu, and this is Sergeant O'Malley," he said. "Oregon State Police. Okay with you if we ask you a few questions?"

"I don't know anything," she said. She wrapped her arms around herself and leaned a hip into the doorway. She was wearing pajama pants and a gray college sweatshirt. Mikie couldn't tell if she had a prosthesis, although her face matched the girl in the video.

"Maybe you know something without realizing it," Mikie said. "I'm very sorry about your friend Paul."

She nodded at the floor.

"Sophie, how old are you?"

"Seventeen."

"Would you rather wait for your mom before you talk to us?" Mikie knew she was taking a risk with the question. But maybe Sophie was the type who'd do anything to leave her mom out of it. (Mikie had been the same—fierce about her privacy, but she missed her mom even more fiercely.)

She had sussed the girl correctly. Sophie shook her head.

"We're trying to find out what happened to Paul," Mikie said.

"Why?" she whispered.

"In case someone did this to him on purpose."

"Nobody would." Her voice was a little stronger now. She looked at Wu. It seemed to Mikie that the girl was avoiding her gaze. Mikie took a tiny step back, letting Wu know he was on.

"Maybe not," he said cheerfully. "Did people like Paul?" Sophie shrugged.

"What's that mean?" Wu asked.

"I don't know how other people feel." There was something spooky about those blue contact lenses. The irises glittered, and the pupils were artificially large. Mikie wondered why she wore them. They were more off-putting than attractive. Of course, she wasn't sure what teenage boys liked.

"You might have an idea," Wu said.

"I don't. Really."

"See, now I think you do," he said, reasonably. "It's not hard to tell, usually. For someone who pays attention, which I bet you are. If someone likes you they do little things, like look at you when you talk and smile from time to time. They might save you a seat at lunch, share their stuff. They don't talk smack about you when you're not around."

"If you're not around then you don't know," she said.

"True that. So who talked smack about Paul when he wasn't around? You?"

"No."

"Didn't somebody? Come on, no one's perfect. Was he a good boyfriend?"

"He wasn't my boyfriend." It was an automatic response, Mikie thought.

"Why not?" Wu asked.

"He was too old for me."

"What, two years? That's not such a big deal."

"My mom thinks so."

"Ah, so your mom wasn't a fan?"

"I didn't say that." She pushed back into her hood, pulling the strings tighter so only the middle of her face showed.

"What did she say about him? Why don't you clear it up for me, if you don't want me to get the wrong idea?"

There was a long pause. Sophie shifted her weight around. Mikie thought she might be favoring her right side. "My mother liked him. You can ask her. But she thought we shouldn't get serious because he's going off to college. I'm still in high school."

"What are you? A junior?"

"Senior."

"True story?" Wu sounded baffled. "You're only a year apart, but Mom thought he was too old for you?"

"Two years. I said."

"Why didn't he go to university last year?" Wu asked.

"I don't know." She was deep in her hoodie now, and Mikie thought Wu had gotten everything he could. But he changed tactics.

"All right. Who here uses insulin?"

"I do," she said, then looked at him with more focus, wary. "You knew that already."

"You're right, I did know. I just wanted to make sure you knew how to tell the truth to a detective. It's a skill not everyone has."

"Is that right?" she said without affect.

"Mm-hmm. So who does your insulin? Your mom?"

"I do it myself."

"That right? You ever loan it out?"

Finally, a reaction—she scowled at Wu. "Why would I do that?"

"Did you or didn't you?"

"No. Of course not." She was standing up straighter now, and there was color in her cheeks. "That's a stupid question."

"Why?"

"Because…it's insulin, it's not like some fun recreational thing. It's dangerous if you don't have diabetes. It's dangerous if you do, even. Your blood sugar can get too low and you feel sick. It's horrible."

"Some people be into that?"

"I don't know. I doubt it."

"Did Paul have access to your insulin?"

She blinked. "Why are you asking me that?" She looked at Mikie, as if for help. "What are you not saying? Why do you care about my insulin? I'm not talking to you anymore."

Mikie said, "That's fine. We can stop talking anytime." Her tone was conciliatory, but she didn't move. She wanted Wu to run with it, if he wanted to.

"Or," Wu said, "we could change the subject. We could talk about other drugs."

Sophie's face grew extremely still. She didn't say anything.

"How does that work, with the insulin? For example, if you're high on Oxy, aren't you worried you might forget a shot?"

A look of fury crossed her face. It was sudden, like the shadow of an airplane passing under the sun. Her hands clenched and unclenched. Wu leaned in closer. He showed her the still photo Colin had printed of her, high, sprawled on a mattress.

"Did Paul take that video? Did your mom find out? Is that what happened, Sophie?"

She glared at him with undisguised hate. She wanted to clock him, Mikie thought.

"Fuck you," she said. "If you want to talk to me, arrest me."

"I just might do that," Wu said to the door as it slammed in their faces.

Chapter 28

July 26, 9:45 p.m.

It took every molecule of courage Isaac possessed to slip away from Adoptees Got Talent. He walked as casually as he could, even gesturing to Hal that he was headed for the bathroom, just in case anyone was watching.

He didn't mind missing the evening's entertainment. It seemed to him that there was a big Paul Anderson–shaped hole at Heritage Camp, and nowhere was it more obvious than at the talent show. But there were still one or two cops milling around, and he didn't want to explain his absence. He was as subtle as possible, leaving when some of the ten-year-olds started break-dancing. The campers were distracted, cheering and clapping in a circle.

Directly south of the infirmary, in the woods and off the path, there was a distinctive, good-sized stump in a stand of firs. Some campers had carved initials in the top. The first shot was completely dark, and he had to fool with the settings, but eventually he had a nice photo of a stump to text to the number from the bathroom wall. He deleted the photo immediately. Then he walked deeper into the woods. When he was in a sufficiently dark cluster of trees, he chose a nice sturdy one and climbed it as quietly as possible. Hal was watching, supposedly, but Isaac neither saw nor heard any sign of him.

Isaac felt like he waited a long time. Away from the fire, he was cold. It began to drizzle. A tree at night was not a silent place; birds and squirrels moved about, bark creaked, wind rustled the pinecones and bounced them to the ground. The feeling of peril heightened his senses, and he could see well in the dark now. Somehow the stump was as clear as it would have been in daylight. He could see the bark in front of him and the holes made by woodpeckers. The spot made him feel claustrophobic, though. He couldn't see the water, or the campfire, or more than a tiny wedge of sky. It was overcast; a starless, uniform gray. Hal wouldn't leave him out here on his own. Would he?

There was movement below—the sound of footfalls on the leaves. Isaac stopped breathing, but as the figure slipped through the forest beneath him, he saw it was only Nathan. Isaac wanted to call out to him to get away. If Nathan got a look at the person who was dealing the Adderall, he could be in danger, but if Isaac called out from the tree, he himself would be exposed. Before he could decide what to do, Nathan pulled something from his pocket and dropped it into the hollow of the stump.

Nathan speed-walked away comically fast, but not fast enough. Hal emerged, a shadow from the trees, and gently took hold of his arm. Nathan startled. Isaac snapped out of his paralysis and climbed down, jumping from a moderately high branch and feeling the shock in his ankles and knees. When he landed, Nathan was running through the trees in the direction of their cabin. Isaac heard him sobbing as he ran.

"It's Nathan? He's your connection?" Isaac whispered. He couldn't believe it.

Hal retrieved the envelope from the tree trunk. His expression was grim, but he opened the packet and tossed a pill in his mouth. He swallowed it dry and sighed. "Apparently so. He doesn't seem to be happy about it, though. Let's get back to AGT. We can regroup at our cabin." He took three steps and vanished into the trees.

They returned—stealthily, separately—to the fireside, just in time to be dismissed for bedtime. They hustled away to their cabin before any of the counselors could notice their total lack of supervision, since Nathan hadn't returned.

"Did you see that coming?" Isaac asked. He struggled to keep his voice low.

"I must admit I did not. Kindly wait here for a moment." They were at the A-frame. "Try to keep the twins out, if you would."

Isaac sat on the steps. Nathan! Other than Hal and himself—and maybe little Eliza—he couldn't think of a less likely drug dealer at camp.

His thoughts were interrupted by the sound of giggling. Someone said "Oh my God" and gasped. He followed the sound and ducked under the cabin. Max and David were huddled over an electronic device, eyes on the screen. "That's messed up," one of them said.

"What are you looking at?" Isaac asked.

Their expressions were identical—glee, mischief, and a touch of wariness.

"Nothing much," Max said.

"Chicks getting high," said David. "Check this." He held the phone out. Isaac found himself staring at a picture of a blond girl smoking something out of a pipe. The cell phone was gray and nondescript. It wasn't Paul Anderson's.

"The next one's so funny," Max said. Isaac scrolled and saw the same girl lying back looking dazed, hair mussed around her head. He had a bad feeling he knew what else was on there.

"Slideshow. Gimme, gimme," David said, bouncing up and down. He grabbed the phone from Isaac and pressed some buttons. Isaac knew that Sophie's picture might pop up anytime. He snatched the phone from David.

"Hey!"

"Just a sec." No Sophie—not yet. "Where'd you get this?"

"We thought it might be yours," Max said.

"Where'd it come from?"

"It was just laying here on the ground. Give it back."

"I will. When?" Isaac demanded.

"Like two minutes ago. Come on, we barely saw anything, they're hilarious."

It occurred to Isaac that Nathan might have dropped it in his rush to get back to the cabin.

"Hang on, I just want to see one thing," he said.

Bingo! Sophie appeared. Isaac couldn't give the phone back. He had to get it away from the twins. "Give me two minutes," he said, and scrambled out from under the cabin. Max was quicker. He punched Isaac in the shoulder, hard; his arm went numb, his fingers opened, and Max grabbed the phone.

"Get your own!" he snapped.

My own, Isaac thought. He fumbled for his own phone and dialed the number he'd used to contact the Adderall connection. The phone in Max's hand buzzed, and he looked down at it.

"What the—?"

Isaac grabbed it again, quick as he could, and sprinted up the stairs and into the cabin, his arm tingling painfully. Nathan was making snuffling noises into his pillow.

Isaac said, "Nathan? Did you drop this?" His arm hurt, and he expected Max and David through the door any second. He kept glancing back over his shoulder. Hal noticed this and inclined his head quizzically. "Twins, incoming," Isaac said.

"Ah."

Nathan sat up, dried his eyes on his sleeve, and saw the phone. "Oh, crap," he said. "I need that. I have to give it back."

"It's the number from the bathroom wall," Isaac told Hal. "And it's not even password protected."

"Yes, that makes sense," Hal said. "Is it disposable? Prepaid, I expect?"

"I don't know," Nathan moaned. "I didn't want to do it."

"Whose phone is it?" Hal asked.

"I can't tell you."

"How absurd. Of course you can."

Isaac wondered what the twins were planning out there.

"I'll get expelled. Or worse," Nathan said.

"All right. Never mind." Hal held up the little bag he'd picked up from the stump. "Do you have a prescription for this?"

"Yes."

"But selling it wasn't your idea, I expect."

"No, of course not."

"Have you taken a good look at this phone, Nathan?" Isaac asked. "All these videos?" He scrolled until he found Sophie, struggled with the decision for a moment, then handed the phone to Hal. He hoped he wasn't blushing. "I've seen that exact video before. On someone else's phone." Those damn sunglasses! He wasn't sure the message had gotten across.

"Nathan," Hal said, "whoever gave you this phone, I won't tell anyone you told me."

"Of course not," Nathan said with bitterness. "Then you'd have to explain why you were buying Adderall."

"That was me, actually," Isaac said.

"You? Why?"

Isaac opened his mouth but closed it again. He didn't really know why.

"You're in an unenviable position, Nathan," Hal said. "I can see that. If you're afraid to tell us, perhaps you'd feel more comfortable talking to the police? I'm sure we can summon an officer promptly. There are still some at camp." His voice was mild, but Nathan looked as though someone had pulled a gun on him.

"You wouldn't."

"Oh, it's not a threat. I thought you might feel safer that way. Since the phone is likely to become evidence in an investigation, having it could be dangerous."

"Investigation? You mean someone knows about the Adderall?"

"Certainly not. I'm referring to the murder."

"What?" Nathan shouted.

"Finally, my brain is working." Hal sighed happily. "Whoever gave you that phone may be complicit in Paul's murder; I see it now. If I were you, I'd want as little to do with this phone—and the person who gave it to you—as possible."

"Paul was murdered?" Nathan cried.

"Of course he was murdered. We've known that for ages."

Eventually the whole story came out, except for the crucial piece: the name. Who owned the phone?

Over the past school year, Nathan had found himself desperate. His school was ultracompetitive, he was in several AP classes, and his parents were determined he should attend one of their alma maters, Stanford or Princeton. A certain person, a "friend" from camp, had offered to write two critical papers and a college essay for a fee. Nathan didn't have much money, but he did have something useful: a diagnosis of ADHD. He offered a moderate number of Adderall tablets; since he rarely took the medication on holidays and weekends, this seemed like a good trade at the time.

But he hadn't counted on the "friend" continuing to hit him up for pills, or threatening him with exposure, or, worse yet, setting up deals that Nathan would have to carry out at enormous risk. "He even arranged proof I cheated," he said. "He wrote the papers, but he also posted them on a website, dated before my papers were due. If anyone goes looking, it looks like I bought them online."

"Devious," Hal said. There was a touch of admiration in his voice. "What about the pictures and videos?"

"Oh, I don't know anything about those. I just have to hang onto the phone for long enough to make the swap."

"Did you look at them, though?" Isaac asked, wondering if he'd seen Sophie.

"No, I just wanted to get it over with."

"You still need to tell us whose phone it is," Isaac said.

"It's all right," Hal said. Isaac couldn't believe it. He made a noise and Hal looked at him. "We'll figure it out."

Nathan protested. "I need to return it. If I don't, he'll come after me. I'm supposed to bring it right back and not let anyone see it."

"How do you get it back to him?"

"Leave it in the bathroom. The handicapped stall. In the little plastic container where, you know, girls are supposed to put their period things."

"Yuck," Isaac said.

"It's not as bad as it sounds. Nobody ever uses that bathroom except—" He stopped abruptly, looking horrified.

And just like that, they knew whose phone it was.

Chapter 29

July 26, 10:00 p.m.

It appeared that no one else at the Tippy Canoe was there to eat. The uniform of the chummy drinkers at the bar seemed to be denim broken up by the occasional black leather jacket and red splash of bandanna. The bar had sprouted a forest of longneck beer bottles. All of this gave Mikie very little confidence in the food, but she was ravenous. A quick stop at home earlier to check in with Jamie and grab a bite to eat had yielded satisfaction on neither front; she could hear Jamie giving a guitar lesson behind the closed door of his "studio," nominally their guest bedroom, and there was nothing in the fridge except eggs, condiments, and beer. Lots of beer. Jamie must have been paid in trade again by one of the pubs he played at. While Wu was outside making a call, she ordered them a couple of BLTs and sweet potato fries from a cheerful bearded fellow in an apron featuring an abstract design rendered in ketchup and grease. It was hard to screw up a BLT in her experience.

Sitting in a dim alcove on red plastic benches, listening to classic rock loud enough to drown out their conversation, she and Wu went through the will. Five minutes after opening the envelope, they knew what material goods Paul Anderson had accumulated in his abbreviated life: a college fund worth $18,000, a used Honda CRX, and a clarinet, all of which he left to his family. He instructed them to use the college fund for his baby sister. He also left the contents of a regular savings account to a place called Wat Po.

Mikie said, "What the heck is Wat Po?" They were practically shouting.

"I think a wat is a dojo or something like that."

Their waiter, arriving with the condiments and flatware, overheard them. "A wat? That's a temple."

"Thanks," Wu said. "You heard of Wat Po?"

"Nope. Our cell service sucks in here, but we have Wi-Fi if you want to google it. Home fries and whiskey ninety-nine, all one word, numerals for ninety-nine."

Mikie plugged the password into her phone and was rewarded with a little loading symbol. "I think we have to consider the suicide angle," she said. "Grace confirmed that both injection sites contained insulin crystals, so he definitely gave himself a shot of it, whether he knew it or not."

Their food arrived. The BLT looked like heaven, nestled into a generous pile of sweet potato fries and coleslaw. She took a bite; it did not disappoint.

"His therapist says no way," Wu said. "She was pissed off when I mentioned it."

"Well, that's not exactly good advertising for a therapist. She might be upset that her treatment failed."

"Epically. But I think that note is a crock. It could mean anything. Maybe it came from a breakup letter. 'Sorry, I know this is hard to understand'—maybe he had some other plans besides college. Maybe he was quitting his counselor job and gave that letter to Mr. Director." He ate a fry. "Mm. Not bad."

"If it was part of a letter, the rest of it should be somewhere," Mikie pointed out.

"Yeah—ashes in the campfire. I think Ty has an agenda. He gave me that impression. But we need to go back to Genevieve."

Mikie wished she'd been present at the interviews. "In a minute. I find the suicide theory hard to swallow for other reasons. For one, he'd have to tamper with his own EpiPen, and/or the nurse's."

"The fridge isn't locked," Wu reminded her. "And she seems flaky. But I agree he probably lacked the know-how."

"So do we. My nurse friend at the ER didn't have any ideas on that front either. But there's another reason I don't like it. As a method of killing yourself, death by anaphylaxis—with or without insulin—has got to be incredibly unpleasant. It would also be cruel to make everyone at camp watch...to let people try to save him and fail. It doesn't fit with anything we've learned about him." She paused to chew and swallow the last bite of her sandwich. The bread had softened up in a puddle of coleslaw liquid, but the lettuce was crisp and, thank goodness, the chef hadn't been stingy with the mayo. "On the other hand, the fact that it was so public may have been attractive because it looked like such an obvious non-suicide. If he did manage to sabotage the EpiPen—or both EpiPens—ingest a peanut butter cup, and go to the dance prepared to collapse and die, his family would get the insurance money. He took out that policy barely a month ago, Wu, and wrote a will."

Wu scoffed. "You ever heard of someone killing himself so someone else gets rich?"

Mikie didn't like it either; she was glad Wu felt the same, but she had to see it through to reject it.

"I've never heard of a nineteen-year-old writing a will, either. Maybe the addiction stuff got the best of him," she said. "Maybe he thought he'd never get better. He'd already gone through all that therapy, and maybe it didn't work. He was getting ready to move out of the family home and didn't trust himself."

Wu finished his sandwich in two bites and shook his head as he chewed and swallowed. "Nah," he finally said. "Try this—we have a very religious family, right? Dad finds drugs, or all that evidence on the laptop, and is furious. They have a new baby now, one of their own, and Paul's becoming more trouble than he's worth. Also, maybe he's getting into Buddhism—why else would he leave money to a temple? That's guaranteed to tick the parents off. And he has life insurance worth $200K. We only have Dad's word that it wasn't his idea all along." Mikie said nothing. She felt sure Mr. Anderson hadn't lied, but it was a good idea to talk through any reasonable theory. "So one or both parents decide to take him out. Either of them have any medical knowledge?"

"Officer Jones says no. She seems very thorough, by the way."

"Too bad she sounds like a Valley girl."

"She's just young," Mikie said. "A lot of girls talk that way. But she's smart, Wu, and she stayed late without being asked tonight, so give her a break." They ate in silence for half a minute, then Mikie went on. "I agree motive is there—not the drugs. I can't see Dad getting angry over something that wasn't Paul's fault. But the insurance, maybe. Don't you think they were truly devastated, though?"

"I'm not sure I can tell. But I think we're wasting time, Mikie. We have a great suspect."

"You mean Genevieve."

"She gave him the damn shot!"

"Only one of them," Mikie reminded him.

"And," Wu went on stubbornly, "she's the only one with a real motive. He had that video of her daughter."

"We don't know if she was aware of that."

"And she had the best opportunity to fuck with the EpiPens. I'm glad we're catching dinner and all that, but I have to tell you, I don't know why we aren't reading her rights this minute."

Mikie shook her head. "Do you know how rare it is for nurses to commit murder? Except for the occasional psychopathic outlier. Charles Cullen types."

"Who's that?"

"A nurse—a guy who murdered elderly patients. He thought he was doing them a favor. He wanted to be called the 'Angel of Death.' By the time they caught him, he'd killed something like forty people at ten different places and had been fired repeatedly. I think we can both agree that doesn't describe Genevieve. Her record is squeaky clean."

Her phone was connected. *Finally!* She touched the internet icon and plugged in "Wat Po." Scrolling down the tiny screen, she read that Wat Po was a Buddhist temple in Bangkok that housed a giant reclining Buddha and the ashes of the royal family from throughout the ages. It also housed several hundred monks. Suddenly it became clear.

"He didn't kill himself," she said. "He *was* going to Thailand. Just like Dollarhyde said."

"Like who?" Wu shouted. The music had been turned up.

"Let's go!" Mikie hollered.

They were outside when Mikie heard her phone buzz with a message. Seven missed calls and three texts!

"Hang on," she told Wu. The most recent text was from Tiffany: "CALL PLZ!" She didn't bother to listen to the voicemails. "Tiffany? What's up?"

"Mikie! I mean, Sergeant—I'm so glad it's you. I found out why Ty Janssen was expelled from the University of Cebu!"

"Tell me."

"Well, I got ahold of the program director, and they didn't want to tell me anything at first? But when I explained who I was they even told me what happened in Oregon, which they didn't know when they admitted him—which they did because he was apparently a really strong student—"

"Officer Jones! Please. What didn't they know?"

The young cop took a deep breath.

"Long story short—he was stealing drugs from the hospital and selling them."

Chapter 30

July 27, 12:15 a.m.

It began to rain. The air smelled of wet cedar and damp rooms that had never been truly clean. The white noise of rain on the roof made Isaac sleepy against his better judgment. But Hal appeared totally alert and focused. He moved his fingers rapidly over his keyboard, his gaze fixed on the laptop screen. He had taken two more of Nathan's pills. When Isaac questioned him, he'd replied, "This is a three-pill problem."

He promised to stay awake and protect them: Isaac from the twins (assuming they ever returned, Isaac had no doubt they'd want to kick his ass) and Nathan from Ty, who might come looking for his special phone. A phone that wasn't even password protected—that's how little he feared Nathan, how untouchable he thought he was. Nathan, wrung out, fell asleep quickly. Isaac closed his eyes and saw motes of light floating behind his eyelids. He realized how exhausted he was, but he didn't want to fall asleep until he understood. He forced his eyes open and spoke in a low voice to Hal.

"So it wasn't Sophie, was it?"

"No."

"Was it really Ty?"

"It would seem so. Get some rest."

Relief was a soporific, and when he closed his eyes, he didn't so much fall asleep as plummet into oblivion. He couldn't have said how much time had passed when a sharp knock on the door jerked him awake. Hal was already shaking Nathan by the shoulder.

"Hide," he said quietly. Nathan, looking terrified, slid under Max's bed. Hal tugged on the covers so they hung to the floor.

But it was only a wet, bedraggled Katie at the door, holding a flimsy polka-dot umbrella.

"Sorry to wake you," she said. "Ty needs Nathan. I guess it's super urgent or something."

"Come in," Hal said. "How kind of you to serve as his emissary."

She gestured at the mud outside. "Wheels don't work in this."

"I'm afraid you got wet for nothing. Nathan isn't here."

"What? But he's your CIT—hey, where are the twins? Aren't they in this cabin?" Now she looked worried. She patted the sleeping bag on Max's bed, right above Nathan. Her feet were inches from his face.

Hal sounded concerned. "They do seem to be missing. But Nathan went to the infirmary. He was feeling unwell. I expect the nurse is keeping him overnight."

"Darn," she said. "I don't know what to do. I guess I'll see if he's there, but maybe I should find Max and what's-his-name first."

"David," Isaac said.

"Thanks, yeah. Any idea where they might be?"

Hal said, "The last time I saw them, they were heading for the gate."

"What! When?"

"Sometime before lights-out. Sorry I can't be more precise. Perhaps Isaac can...?"

"I'm not sure what time it was." Isaac's mouth was dry.

"I assumed their parents were picking them up. I do hope they weren't planning anything nefarious," Hal added with a concerned look.

"Oh my God," Katie said. "This is a disaster! Send Nathan to the lodge if he comes back, would you? And the twins too, obviously."

"Of course. Happy hunting."

And she was gone, disappearing into the rain. It was now torrential, not only noisy, but impossible to see through for more than a few feet. Hal was putting his shoes on.

"What should I do?" Nathan whispered. "I told you he'd come after me!"

"Witness protection is in order, I think," Hal said. "Let's go. No, Isaac, no flashlight."

"I should just give the phone back," Nathan said. "I'll go myself. There's no reason for you two to get involved." He was trying to be brave, but his voice was shaky.

"Out of the question," Hal said. "The phone is evidence." He tapped the phone with his thumbs. They heard the noise of an outgoing text, then he slipped the phone into a pocket.

"Who are you texting?" Isaac asked.

"We need to go now."

They didn't have umbrellas. Isaac followed Hal, who walked faster than anyone he'd ever seen. "Where are we going?"

"Someplace safe for Nathan."

They were headed away from the lake, toward Walden Cabin. Isaac jogged to keep up.

"Tanya's? Why would she help us?"

They ran up to the porch and stood dripping. The overhang provided some protection from the rain above, but the wind blew enormous droplets sideways into their faces and bare legs. "Isaac. No offense is intended when I say you won't learn anything with your mouth open." He rapped on the door.

Thirty seconds later, the door opened. Tanya looked awful; she was pale, and her hair hung lank around her face. But she made an effort to smile at them.

"It must be something that can't wait."

"May we come in, please?" Hal asked.

She could hardly say no, Isaac thought. But she hesitated. "You want to come in?"

"If we could. It's a bit wet out here."

She opened the door. "All right," she said rather loudly. "You may come in."

The room seemed small with the four of them inside, especially with the dividing screen. Tanya closed the front door. She crossed her arms over her chest and said, "I assume you'll explain."

Hal looked at Nathan, who fidgeted. His glasses fogged up, and water dripped off his nose. "Oh, go ahead. It doesn't matter now."

"Nathan finds himself in possession of something that belongs to someone else. Something highly incriminating," Hal explained.

"Really," she said, raising her eyebrows. "That sounds like a reason to turn it over to a counselor. Or better yet, the director."

Nathan gasped. "You can't! Please, just let me stay here. Just for a few hours."

"Nathan," Tanya said. "I can't have a camper in here overnight. It's totally inappropriate. And it's the middle of the night, boys. What is it that's so incriminating?"

No one answered. Tanya looked at them each in turn. "I think I'd better call Ty."

"No! Not Ty," Nathan begged.

"Katie, then."

Isaac looked at Hal, who made no move to go and said nothing. He just stood looking at Tanya as she picked up the phone.

"We know who killed Paul," Isaac blurted. She stopped dialing. Hal still said nothing, regarding Tanya with an air of interest.

She flinched. "No one killed him. It was an allergic reaction."

"Then why are the police asking so many questions?" Isaac said. He felt incredibly bold. It was an unfamiliar sensation, but he liked it. "They're treating it as a murder. That detective talked to you, too, for a long time. Did he act like it was an accident?"

Her voice was steady. "I'm sure the police know what they are doing, boys. They just...need to rule things out. If you have information, you should give it to them."

"Oh, I intend to," Hal said. "Any minute now. Should I tell them about the stolen babies, too?"

Tanya didn't move. "What?"

"And that one of them was your son?"

She sat down.

"Don't worry," Hal said. "I don't think the police need to know about that, actually. It isn't relevant to the current situation. But we do need a place to stash Nathan, and I do have some questions, if you don't mind. Oh, and Isaac and Nathan have no idea what I'm talking about."

And then Paul Anderson stepped around the screen that served as a room divider. "Who was it?" he asked. "Who killed my brother?"

Chapter 31
July 26, 11:00 p.m.

Wu was on his way to Judge Kelly's house in southwest Portland to get a warrant to search Ty's room, cell phone, and computer. Mikie was headed back to Adventist to meet with Rachel, who had called sometime during their hurried dinner at the Tippy Canoe. She sounded excited in the voicemail: "Mikie! I have an idea about your EpiPen. Call or come by, I'm still at work. Hurry!"

Mikie's ears were still ringing from the ridiculous volume of the music, and Bob Seger's voice echoed hoarsely in her head. She turned off the radio. Logically, she knew Wu was right. Genevieve was the most obvious culprit, and the incriminating video of her only child could have provided a motive. But Mikie was relieved to have another scenario. Maybe she didn't want to believe a fellow nurse had been so calculating, so cruel.

Whatever her personal feelings, though, it was undeniable that the camp director made a great suspect. Ty Janssen had mentioned insulin, directed them to a probably phony suicide note, and had a history that could explain the video on Paul Anderson's phone and the other drug-related evidence on his computer. How would that have led to murder, though? Blackmail, vengeance, shame—she supposed there were plenty of ways it could have gone. Furthermore, the program director at the University of Cebu had confirmed that Janssen had plenty of experience with medical equipment and was as likely as anyone else to know how to sabotage an EpiPen—if such a thing were possible. Their pre-med program included several hospital shifts, where the students functioned as nursing assistants on graveyard. "He was an excellent student, but it was clear he didn't know right from wrong. It was very upsetting to us, especially after we learned about the issues at university." The man on the phone sounded tinny, and there was a slight delay, but his English was perfect, his tone unmistakably regretful.

Mikie said, "All we know is that he was expelled."

"He told us it was an issue of plagiarism. Unintentional. We don't automatically reject students with that kind of history. We like to give second chances. But after the incident, when we looked further, it turned out to be worse than that—he was selling term papers. There was also a report of extortion. He threatened to expose the person who bought work from him and demanded money. This young man, unfortunately, turned out to be a bad actor. He was certainly remorseless when we discovered his behavior."

Also, how could he have known about the insulin if he hadn't been a party to their conversation? There were only so many explanations. Maybe Paul Anderson really had discussed suicide with Ty; maybe insulin really had come up. She didn't believe their victim had killed himself, but it wasn't totally out of the question. Could Ty have known somehow about the blood-sugar level or the insulin in the injection site? They hadn't released that information, but could he have overheard an interview? Genevieve was the only person they'd asked about the insulin—no, that wasn't true—Wu had asked Sophie too. Either of them could have mentioned it to Ty, although Wu had talked to Ty before they met with Sophie. The third possibility, of course, was that he knew about it because he was the one who'd put it there. But how?

She hoped Rachel might be able to solve that particular problem. She parked and hurried to the ER, where she waited impatiently behind a stressed-looking woman with two toddlers as she tried to get the clerk's attention. Finally, the clerk glanced at Mikie. "Are you here for Rachel? She says go on back." The clerk pressed a button, and the twin doors to the patient care area opened wide. Mikie walked into the bright chaos and saw Rachel waving to her from the other end. She walked past patients on gurneys who lay blinking up at the ceiling and past the counters cluttered with laptops and papers. She sensed faces turning to her with interest as she followed Rachel into the break room.

"This won't take long. You're going to love it." Rachel grinned.

"You figured it out?"

"I had to do an I.O. placement earlier—poor kid—and voila! It came to me. You ever use an I.O. needle?"

"I don't even know what it is."

"They've only gotten popular the past couple years. It's an intraosseous needle. You can infuse fluids into someone even if they have lousy veins or are too dehydrated to stick one. All the ERs have them."

Genevieve worked at a pediatric ER, Mikie recalled. She felt a little rush of excitement. "They'd have them at a peds ER, then?"

"Absolutely. They use them more than anywhere else."

"You put it into a bone?"

"Yup, the tibia. It's a fat, stout needle and you stick it in like a dart," Rachel said.

"Ouch."

"I want to try it on your EpiPen."

Mikie pulled it out of her pocket. "Please do."

"Now, what you want to know is whether a person can sabotage it and turn it into an insulin pen, right? Even if this works, I'm not sure it's possible. There isn't a button to depress the plunger. You press it to the thigh—"

"I know how it works. Can you get the epi out and put the insulin in?"

"Let's find out." Rachel took hold of the bright yellow canister. She aimed what looked like a hot glue gun at it. The needle shot out and penetrated the plastic instantly. "And Bob's your uncle."

"Jesus. Can you get anything out of it?"

"I'll try." Rachel attached a small plastic syringe and withdrew a couple of cubic centimeters of clear liquid. Mikie watched as the plunger meekly moved down inside the unit. Rachel placed the full plastic syringe on the table. "Now let's see if we can add something to it. This should be the same viscosity as insulin, which is pretty watery." She picked up a different syringe, carefully attached it to the 10 needle in the EpiPen, and as she depressed the plunger, they watched the flange inside the EpiPen rise.

"Of course there's a hole in the side now. That would have to be plugged."

"With what?" Mikie wondered.

"Superglue was my idea. We have some in the ER, although we call it something different and we charge more for it." She put a glove on and squeezed glue from a small tube onto her fingertip. As she withdrew the needle, she followed it with a glob of glue. "It will dry within seconds. If you're a bad guy and you sand that lump of glue down, probably no one will notice the hole."

It was done. Mikie regarded the EpiPen, amazed. "Rachel, you're a genius. You're wasted here—you should become a detective."

"Maybe I will. Do you really think this was murder?"

"It would help if we could find that fucking EpiPen," she said. "But yes, I do. A clever one."

"But not," Rachel said with satisfaction, "as clever as us."

Chapter 32

July 27, 1:30 a.m.

Isaac knew he was going to faint. It had happened to him before; there were black spots in his peripheral vision, his lips felt numb, and the voices around him were oddly muffled. He didn't want to fall over, so he sat on the floor and awkwardly put his head down. Although his eyes were closed, he sensed everyone standing over him and felt their concern with embarrassment.

"I'm fine," he said. As he opened his eyes to Tanya's kind and worried face, he had the fleeting thought that she looked a lot stronger—more like herself—than she had in the past couple of days.

"How about a cup of tea?" she said.

Hal was peering over Tanya's shoulder. "Excellent restorative. Good idea. Nathan can help you," he said pointedly.

"Yeah, sure," Nathan said, jumping up to help Tanya.

"I saw Paul," Isaac said. But Hal was shaking his head.

"No. His brother." Isaac looked again and, of course, Hal was right. The young man with his arms akimbo, surveying the rest of them seriously, was not Paul. There was a strong resemblance, but he wasn't as tall, and his skin was browner. When he spoke, Isaac saw that one front tooth was chipped.

"I'm Will," he said with a slight accent. "My mother calls me Mai. Sorry about frightening you."

"I'm not frightened," Isaac said. "I was just...I guess I'm tired. And surprised."

"First things first," Tanya said. "Isaac, are you able to sit in a chair? Your tea is almost ready. And I want you to eat some cookies."

There was a minute or two of awkward shuffling while Isaac got situated. He nibbled at a cookie, feeling embarrassed. Not only because he had nearly fainted, but because he'd thought Tanya and Paul were—well, not exactly mother and son. He was glad he'd never mentioned his suspicions to Hal, and even gladder when Hal clapped his hands together and everyone turned to him instead.

"Very good," Hal said. "Isaac, you look better already. Questions, anyone? I have a few myself, if no one else does."

"No," said Tanya firmly. "I think I will go first. First of all, what do you know—or think you know?"

"Maa," said Will who spoke rapidly, softly. *Maa* was Thai for Mother, Isaac recalled suddenly. When he was young, his parents had made an attempt to learn some Thai with him, taking him to lessons on Saturday mornings. Isaac heard Will say what sounded like "pea jai," and he knew *pii* meant big brother, but nothing else was comprehensible. Tanya responded in rapid Thai that sounded like music with its lilting tones. Then she said, "What Mai wants can wait. Of course, he wonders what really happened to Paul."

Nathan burst out, "This is—I can't...I feel like I'm dreaming. Am I?"

"No one is privy to the whole story, although I have some of the pieces," Hal said. "Isaac, somewhat less. I believe that Paul was your son and that he was taken from you. And you found him somehow, not terribly long ago. I'm not sure how. Some of this is guessing."

"Go on," Tanya said. She was very still.

"You're not Thai, correct? Khmer, I think, ethnically—probably from Cambodia. And you may have lived in Thailand, but you weren't adopted from there. At least, not to the United States. There were only 235 adoptions from Thailand in the entire decade around when you said you were adopted, and none of them fit with your date of birth. There was no reason to lie about your birthday in the Heritage Camp brochure. And you didn't go to high school in Ohio, like your profile says—neither your name nor your photo appears in any Ohio yearbook."

She interrupted. She looked shocked, almost angry. "Wait. I still don't understand. What made you so suspicious about me? No one has ever questioned me like this."

"You didn't come to the beach the night Paul died," Hal said simply.

"I was sick."

"People needed you—just being sick wouldn't have kept you away. But you were too upset, and you thought it might make the kids feel worse to see the camp therapist in such a state. Why would you be so upset unless there was something more between you and Paul? When I considered what that might be, I noticed the resemblance. After that it was a matter of simple confirmation." Isaac thought of his own suspicions and hoped no one noticed him blush.

"You were right," she said. Her shoulders sagged, but she kept her head held high. Mai came over and took her hand. "But how?"

"Well, mostly research and observation. My facial-recognition program—which I used to search the Ohio database—confirmed my suspicion that you and Paul might be related."

"A computer program can tell you that?" she asked. Nathan's jaw hung open.

"Well, mine can. It's not as good as DNA testing, but it is a lot faster, and quite reliable for first-degree relatives. That's been my project for several months now," he added modestly. "I had an internship at Intel last year."

Genotypes and phenotypes! Isaac thought. But he must have said it aloud, because everyone looked at him. Nathan was shaking his head. His lips formed the word "unbelievable."

"Very good, Isaac." Hal smiled. "Oh, and that article you wrote for the Hague Adoption Convention filled in the missing pieces."

Isaac said, "The one you showed me? The one about the…"

Hal was looking at Tanya as he answered. "Stolen babies. Yes. Great article, by the way, Tanya, well done."

"That article hasn't even been published. It's sitting in a file in the Netherlands," she said.

"And in the Heritage International database," Hal said. "It's part of your employee file. That required a bit of mid-level hacking. Nothing too challenging. The Hague has better security," Hal explained.

"But…it can't be! I didn't submit it to Heritage."

"Well, someone found it. Does anyone else at Heritage have a connection to the Hague?"

She nodded slowly. "Heritage has a big stake in how the recommendations turn out. The director is on their board. But I can't believe they saw the paper and hired me. It's very critical of international adoption."

"A 'blistering critique,' to be precise," Hal said. "But the file also mentions your counseling work with adoptees, several glowing recommendations and all that."

Mai said, "Who cares about this? I'm sorry, Maa, but I want to know about my brother."

Hal shuffled his feet. He looked uncomfortable. "Well, I could be wrong on that particular detail," he said.

Tanya shook her head slowly. "You're incredible," she said.

"Would you mind filling in the blanks?" Hal asked politely.

"I'm not sure that's a good idea," she said, looking around at all of them.

"None of us will say anything," Isaac assured her.

"No, definitely not," Nathan agreed. "And…I don't know what you're going to say, but stolen babies? I mean, that sounds important to us all. As adoptees."

Mai touched her shoulder and spoke quietly in Thai. He seemed to be persuading her.

Hal said, "If it's too painful—"

"No," she said, deciding. "Living it was painful. Telling it—that doesn't scare me anymore. Mai and I went through so much together. I'll answer your questions if you'll answer his."

"I prefer not to be responsible for vigilantism. This young man—hello, by the way; I'm Hal Shaw—appears to have martial arts training, does he not?"

"Mai won't hurt anyone. He is a disciplined person." Isaac wasn't so sure about that, but Mai, or Will, stood quietly while his mother spoke.

Tanya was born Than in a small village in Cambodia. Her parents had been schoolteachers, and her grandfather a professor of psychology. But by the time she was born, the intellectuals had been killed or broken by the Khmer Rouge, and her family was barely surviving as inexperienced subsistence farmers far from the city.

When she was eleven she was sold and brought to Thailand. An uncle had a connection and was supposedly eager to help her find work. She thought she would be a domestic worker in the home of some wealthy people. She planned to send money home, but—

"The less I can say about that time, the better. It was—slavery is the right word." She never saw her parents again.

Sometime later, she wasn't sure when, a Thai man came to the house and offered to rescue her, paying off the people who kept her locked up. He brought her to his home outside of the city, which seemed like a refuge at first. She had her own room and was allowed to talk with other girls in the house. "But they were strange and always sleepy. I later learned they were opium addicts. They told me to do what King said and not to make trouble. I tried. But he abused me." She got pregnant, and after she gave birth—isolated at King's house, in terrible pain and fear—he took her baby boy. "He said Jai Yen would be going to America and would have a good life. I should be happy for him. At that moment I realized the truth: I was part of a baby factory." When she became pregnant again, she escaped by complaining about stomach pains until he allowed her to go to a clinic. A Thai nurse helped her. "She spoke my language because she'd worked at the border of my country, in the refugee camps. She saved my life, because I would have died before going through that again."

She gave birth to another boy, Mai, whom she struggled to raise alone. "I was so poor. I couldn't go back to my family, even if I'd had the money and papers to get there—there was too much shame. I could barely feed the two of us. Mai asked me to send him to fight school—some of his friends had gone. They would feed and house the boys and teach them Muay Thai."

"Thai boxing," Mai said. He flexed his hands, and Isaac noticed there were bandages on his palms. He wondered what had happened.

"I didn't want to send him—they exploit the fighters, and gamblers bet money on them. But I had very little choice. I sent him away until I could make a plan to improve our lives. In Thailand, I would always be afraid of King and his thugs. And I wanted to find Jai Yen—that's Paul's original name." She got to the United States not through adoption, but by finding a husband. She married an American man she met through an online service. After visiting, he agreed she could bring her son and even paid for all their papers. Everything was for sale in Bangkok, including passports that transformed them into Thai nationals. And there were English lessons. She was a good student. "I had already been sold twice. This time, I arranged everything myself." Mai was ten by then, almost the age she'd been when she left Cambodia. She changed his name to her favorite English word: "will."

In Ohio, she felt safe for the first time. But she constantly thought about her first child. When she saw Asian children with their white parents, her heart seemed to stop. She learned about the adoption community and realized it made sense to search there. She needed an in, a professional role. Counseling seemed like a good idea. "I wanted to help people, all the stolen babies especially. I wasn't pretending about that. But I wanted to find my son more." She went to community college, transferred to a university, and went straight to graduate school. She was diligent. "The marriage didn't survive," she said. "He is a nice man. But his idea of a wife didn't include a master's degree."

She specialized in adoption issues. Once she didn't have a husband to contradict her story, she presented herself as an adoptee, making her a more attractive candidate for positions like the one at Heritage. In graduate school, she also became involved with the Hague Adoption Convention, whose mandate was to decrease corruption in adoption. "They want to stop the child selling. Too late for me, but it's important for others."

Mai always knew he had an older brother. When he was old enough, Tanya told him the truth: that Jai Yen was somewhere in America and she wanted to find him. After Will finished high school, they traveled to Thailand together. Her official reason for going was to carry out research for the Hague, which made it possible for her to visit adoption agencies, ask sensitive questions, and identify birth mothers, many of whom she interviewed. She also hoped it might lead her to the man who sold her son.

"Mai was amazing. So brave. He pretended to be interested in the girls on Sukhumvit Five, where King found me. Then he asked them questions. He did this over and over until he tracked down some associates of the men who sold me. Finally, someone mentioned an 'orphanage' that had been very profitable but went out of business just months earlier. It was very close to the house where King kept me and the other girls, and it was supposedly connected to a church in Oregon." Tanya wasn't able to connect the women with their children, or even with the same orphanage. But a visit to the American church in Oregon confirmed there were several teenagers adopted from Thailand among the congregation. None was younger than thirteen, so she realized either the supply or the demand had waned.

Isaac surprised himself by asking, "Including Paul—I mean, Jai Yen?"

She nodded. Her eyes were shining. "As soon as I saw him, I knew."

"When did you tell him?" Hal asked.

"I didn't." Her voice cracked. "When I visited the church, I introduced myself as a counselor working with adoptees. His parents approached me. Before I ever saw him, they told me things about him...it made it difficult to tell him the truth about who I was. It might have embarrassed him. And I was just so happy to see him that I took what I could get."

"What was his main problem?" Hal asked.

"I don't want to say. It doesn't matter now."

"How did he find out?" Hal asked.

"How do you know he did?"

"I don't want to say," Hal said. "It doesn't matter now."

Tanya smiled wryly. "He saw Mai coming out of my cabin. Mai was very careful, but Paul came at an unexpected time, and, seeing the resemblance, he was upset and confused. Obviously, I should have told him sooner. I tried to explain what had happened, how I had searched. That he was stolen, not given up. That there were other babies in the same situation."

"Including Sophie," Hal said, "if I am not mistaken."

She shook her head. "I can't tell you that. Even if I knew, I would never."

"Did Paul know?"

"At first he didn't believe that so many babies were abducted rather than given up freely to be adopted. He insisted on seeing my paperwork...how could I refuse him anything? He went through everything: interviews with the mothers, photos of that same phony orphanage, even receipts for cash payments—the criminals were so confident they'd never be caught because no one would listen to the women. Finally, he believed."

But Isaac barely heard. He had stopped listening when he heard the name. "Sophie?" he said. "Sophie was kidnapped too?"

Hal said, "Tanya? Who started the fire?"

She shook her head, shrugged, and turned to Isaac. "All the babies were taken from their mothers shortly after they were born. All the mothers I've met say they had no choice. The police ignored them, or worse. One of the mothers actually spent time in jail for making 'false accusations.' Others, the criminals dealt with in their own way. Most women just gave up."

Isaac's mind raced. "Were they all stolen, though?" he said. "I mean...I have a picture of my birth mother...how could that be, if..."

"If you were stolen? I don't know, Isaac, but it is possible."

"But my family doesn't go to that church. We don't go to any church."

"The baby thieves will work with anyone. They don't care who. They just want money. It is a business. A profitable business."

"They burned the papers," Hal asked, "didn't they?"

Will—Mai—raised his bandaged hands and said, "I saved what I could. Now it's time to tell me what I want to know."

There was a knock on the door.

Chapter 33

July 27, 2:30 a.m.

Mikie stood out in the wet and peered into the cabin. "I know it's the middle of the night. I got a text asking me to come here." Tanya Miller stood in the doorway, looking pale but composed. Three bewildered teenagers sat looking at her: the slight, pretty boy was probably Isaac; the chubby one looked terrified behind his thick glasses; and the boy with the short-cut afro, wearing wraparound sunglasses and an air of adult poise, matched Wu's description of Hal Shaw. And a young man who looked almost exactly like Paul Anderson stood in front of a lamp. Backlit, it was hard to see his face, the lamp throwing a corona of light around him. But she saw bandages on his hands and knew immediately that this was Anderson's imposter. She deliberately didn't react, though her pulse raced. "You're all up late," she said. "Or early."

Tanya stepped aside for her to enter the cabin.

Hal said, "We may have some insights to share with you, Detective. Perhaps you and I should speak in private?"

"You're the one who texted me?" she said.

"Affirmative."

That meant he had the phone, which made him a suspect. "How did you get my number?"

"From your colleague, Detective Wu."

She very much doubted that Wu had given out her cell number, but she let it go. "And who are you?"

"Hal Shaw. At your service." He bowed, apparently unironically.

"How old are you?"

"Sixteen."

"You need a responsible adult with you."

Tanya said, "I can do that." Mikie thought she looked worried. What was she afraid Hal might say?

"There's no need, Detective," he said coolly. "I'm an emancipated minor. You can look me up, if you like."

An emancipated minor who was adopted? If that was true, it was interesting. "All right. Let's step onto the porch."

"The boathouse is likely to be more private as well as drier," he suggested.

"The rest of you," she said, "don't go anywhere."

She followed him down the path toward the water. She had to walk faster than was comfortable to keep up; it was irritating. And she wanted to keep the cabin in view in case the Anderson look-alike decided to skip out. From the dock, she could still see the front porch. "This is private enough. What is it you want to tell me?"

"I think you know Paul Anderson's death was no accident. Yes?"

"Go on." She wished he would take those silly glasses off. Between those and the preternatural poise, she couldn't get a sense of his motives or whether he was being honest.

"I believe," he said, "I have identified the culprit. Or at least a likely one."

"And that would be who?"

"I hesitate to share the information without some assurances."

She resisted a slight urge to smack the glasses off his face. Instead she spoke sternly. "If you have information pertinent to the investigation, you'd better tell me. Not to mention how you found it."

"Telling you will uncover certain misdeeds and secrets…I assure you they are unrelated to your investigation."

Why did people always think they knew that? "I decide whether they're related. And I'm not promising anything. How did you get the phone?"

He sighed. "My friend was involved in a scheme, much against his will, that involved using the phone to make contact."

"And who owns it?" Mikie asked.

"I want to know there will be no legal consequences for my friend."

"I can't tell you that."

"I can wear a wire," he said. There was barely suppressed excitement in his voice. "I can trap the murderer."

For Christ's sake, she thought. "Catching killers is my job. Not yours. And it's very dangerous."

"I assure you I am in no danger. But while this person is at large, other people may be."

"Who is it, Hal?"

He sighed again, then handed her a generic-looking smartphone. "Turn it on and you'll see a short video of a friend of mine. I think it came from someone here at camp. Isaac saw the identical video on Paul's phone a few days before he died."

She glanced at the phone, taking in the same image she'd been studying for clues. As annoying as this kid was, she was intrigued. "Whose phone is this?"

"Ty Janssen's. He's the camp director."

"What makes you think this has anything to do with murder?"

"Sophie—that's her, there—is underage, obviously. Additionally, there are pictures and videos of other kids using drugs. Ty was also engaged in academic fraud, selling term papers to kids and then blackmailing them—although I don't know if the phone proves that. I think Ty was afraid Paul was getting ready to turn him in."

"Why?" she asked. *It fits*, she thought, but she kept her voice skeptical.

"He was blackmailing Nathan. He and Paul had argued the night before—Sophie heard them. I saw him leave some papers on your partner's car, which hardly seems innocent. And they were close enough for Ty to deliberately expose him to peanuts—that is what happened, right?"

Instead of answering, she asked, "How do I know this isn't your phone? For all I know, you took the video."

"Nathan can corroborate what I tell you, as long as you make sure he's safe—from Ty, who's already come looking for him, and from legal consequences."

"Was it you who faxed me a note about blackmail?"

"No. But that's interesting," he said, frowning. "Maybe Ty felt that he was being blackmailed, or maybe he was considering blackmailing Paul. Either way, he definitely wants this phone back. Every moment it's out of his hands, he grows more dangerous."

"Why did Nathan have it?"

"He borrowed it to send a quick text."

If this clever oddball was right—assuming he was telling the truth—why hadn't Ty disposed of the phone? "Why would he loan it to Nathan?"

"He needed Nathan to carry out a deal. The details are unsavory."

"Hal," she said warningly.

"Fine. A drug deal—with me, in fact."

"That seems incredibly risky."

"Hubris, I believe," Hal said, adding, "I wonder who sent that fax. It might have been Katie. She was acting a little strangely earlier. Maybe Ty has something on her too."

Hubris was consistent with what they knew about Ty, all right. Expelled from college only to get up to even worse shenanigans someplace else. "If you're right and Ty's a killer, you've made a target out of yourself and your friends by holding onto this phone."

"I'm not afraid on my own behalf. But you'll remember I did text you, Detective."

"One more question," she said. "Who's the young man who looks like Paul?"

"I think you'd better ask Tanya. That's not my information to share."

This kid made her curious. She asked, "Why do you wear those glasses all the time?"

"Will you let me wear a wire?"

Out of the question, she thought. But she conceded. "I'll ask the district attorney." She could always tell him the DA said no.

In reply, he took off his sunglasses. She looked at his mismatched eyes and nodded.

"Esotropia," he said lightly as he slid the shades back on. "Caught too late to remedy. But I see perfectly well. I daresay I see things other people don't."

Chapter 34

July 27, 3:15 a.m.

Isaac could just see the tops of their heads as the detective and Hal stood by the boathouse, hashing something out. The rain had slowed considerably, and there was mist hanging above the lake. Nathan paced on the porch of Tanya's cabin.

"What could they be saying?" he kept asking.

"Don't worry," Isaac said. Again. "He won't say anything about the pills."

"Oh, I know he wouldn't throw me under the bus. Not on purpose. But what if she figures it out anyway?"

"I don't think that's her priority."

"And even worse," Nathan went on, "Ty's going to find out that people know. I can't win. Either the police find out, or Ty does. I'm screwed." He was in tears again. "How did everything get so messed up? No, never mind, I messed it up myself. I never should have bought those papers. I'm so stupid!"

Isaac wondered if everyone lived like this—undercover. Hal with his shades, Sophie with her contacts. And him. "You're not stupid," he said, feeling the words were inadequate. "Everyone does things they're ashamed of. Everyone has secrets."

"Not like this."

He could have said, *Yeah they do, worse than this.* He could have said, *Oh yeah? Let me tell you a little something about myself.* But he didn't. Maybe he didn't have the courage. Or maybe, he rationalized, he needed to save his courage for later.

When Hal and the detective returned to the cabin, it was nearly dawn. Isaac thought they both looked a little bit aggravated; they must have compromised on something.

"May I explain to my friends?" Hal asked her, sounding almost meek.

"Go right ahead. I have some questions for you, Ms. Miller." Her glance flickered to Mai, then back to Tanya. Tanya nodded, looking nervous but composed. "And I'll have to make a couple calls." Detective O'Malley gestured to Tanya and Mai, and they entered the cabin while the others gathered on the porch around Hal.

Ty was the likely suspect, Hal explained. The detective wouldn't say what all their reasons were for suspecting him, except that the killer had some medical training, and that apparently implicated Ty. The business in drugs and school papers gave Ty something to hide at all costs. But there was no real evidence that he'd killed Paul. They needed a confession.

"I thought of something," Nathan said. "He's afraid of ghosts, remember?"

"Go on."

"Remember how he freaked out about the ghost stories? And we have Will—or Mai, who looks just like Paul…"

"Ah, the film," Hal said.

"Exactly!"

"You could superimpose an image?" Hal asked.

"No problem."

"A ghostly image?"

"Totally." Nathan grinned.

"If Will agrees, we can add him to the film and show Ty," Hal said slowly.

"This is very *Scooby-Doo*!" Nathan said.

"You can't have Mai speak," Isaac reminded them. "He sounds completely different."

"He won't have to. Let's propose it to him."

When Mai and Tanya emerged about ten minutes later, Hal went over the plan again. Mai was willing, but with one caveat. "If I help you with this, and it is true he killed my brother, I want five minutes alone with him."

Tanya said, "I don't know. This sounds dangerous." Mai touched her hand and spoke quietly in Thai. She looked at all of them again. "Can you be careful enough?" she asked. "Isaac? Do you feel safe?" He nodded. "We'll see what the police officer thinks," she said.

Then they had to explain it to the detective. When she finished her phone call, they all filed into the cabin. She listened carefully without interrupting. From the expression on her face, Isaac was sure she would reject the whole idea. But she tapped an index finger on the table and was silent for almost a whole minute.

Finally she said, "I have...some questions. First, are you serious? I can't imagine the DA will go for this, but could you actually do it?"

"Yes," Nathan hurried to say. "I mean, the video part is no problem."

"Second, is he really that afraid of ghosts?"

"He is," Hal said.

"And who's going to show him this video? How can I be sure they'll be safe? If you're right and he's the killer, he might lash out."

"No need to worry about that, Sergeant. He can't hurt me," Hal said.

"I will be there also," said Mai. "If he confesses..."

"No," the detective said firmly. "If you—or anyone here—thinks they're going to confront our suspect, I will make absolutely sure you stay out of the way, in custody if necessary. Understood?"

"Detective," Tanya said, "none of us will interfere. We all want the same thing: justice for Paul."

"For your son," the detective said.

Tanya nodded. Her expression was troubled. "Did Ty really do this terrible thing?"

"If this works, you'll have an answer soon." She went outside with her phone, and when she came back, looking unhappy, she said, "Somehow, the DA agreed. Probably half asleep. So it's a go. Hal, Detective Wu will set up your wire when he arrives. Let's go over the plan."

As the sun rose, Nathan used his phone to take some photos and videos of Mai. Isaac walked quickly back to their cabin to retrieve Hal's laptop so that Nathan could do the film editing at Tanya's. He was glad to see that Max and David had returned, but even gladder that they slept through his brief visit; his arm was still sore. As he quietly left the cabin, he saw that the earth was torn up. It looked like someone had ridden a bike—no, two bikes—right up to their door. *Wheels*, he thought with sudden clarity. Ty had come looking himself, in the rain.

He shuddered and ran back to Tanya's. The rain had stopped, the sky was growing light and the air smelled clean, but none of that could allay his sense of peril. He should have been tired, but he felt the opposite, nerved up and jittery. When he saw Tanya standing straight and still in the morning light, he felt better for some reason.

"Come talk with me," she said, patting the porch glider.

"I need to give them this."

"Afterward, then."

He gave Nathan the computer and went back outside.

"Um, people will be up soon," he said to Tanya.

"That's all right," she said as he sat beside her. "Do you have that picture of your birth mother you were talking about?"

Isaac pulled out his wallet. He wasn't really sure why he carried the photo around. It was in a plastic sheath to keep it safe, though there was a copy in his scrapbook at home. A woman who looked quite a lot like him sat in a pink room, in a metal folding chair, with a baby on her lap. He recognized his own worried expression in the tiny squished face.

She smiled at him. "You were a lovely baby."

"Thanks…I guess. Do you think, I mean, does it look like…was I one of the stolen babies?"

She looked closely at him. "I don't know," she said. "This picture can't tell me that. It doesn't look like the others, though. And Heritage arranged a lot of legitimate adoptions."

"That's good, I guess," he said. It was disorienting to imagine anything else.

"How are things with your parents?" she asked.

He reeled but tried to sound normal, even chipper. "Great. They're, you know, kind of protective."

"Do you think they might be open to talking about this?"

"I don't know." His mom was softhearted and wept over small, routine injustices done to others. His dad often hid the newspaper when there were earthquakes, hurricanes, or sweatshop disasters with heartbreaking photos. "I don't know if I'd even want to."

"Okay. Well, if you feel like talking about it sometime, please get in touch with me."

A thought suddenly struck him like a blow: if his birth mother did look, she'd never find him. She'd be looking for a girl.

Chapter 35

July 27, 4:05 a.m.

Mikie had never seen Wu looking so put upon, but at least he was calm about it, unlike her former partner who used to slam doors and call her a stubborn bitch. He closed the car door carefully, with restraint. When he finally spoke, his voice was low and controlled.

"Help me understand," he said. "We've ruled out the nurse for some reason. I have the warrant for Janssen's computer—a warrant I obtained with some trouble, by the way, from a cranky judge in the middle of the night—but we're not going to use it. Instead we're sending in a kid—a very weird kid—for some kind of sting operation."

"That's about the size of it."

"Mikie, this is crazy."

"You know a confession is better than anything we're going to pull off the computer. He won't have put anything in there about killing Paul Anderson."

Wu shook his head, looking at the lake. "Okay. Okay. You want a confession. You want the drama—"

"Excuse me?"

"—and you can't see who our best suspect is because she's a nurse. It's the truth, Mikie."

Mikie felt her temper begin to flare, but she could see his point and tamped it down. "Feel free to disagree with me, Detective—"

"Oh, I do."

"—as long as you do your job while you're at it. Hal gets the wire."

Wu was still shaking his head. "This is a mistake. We could at least use a professional. Sonia Madison is available, and she looks about fourteen."

"Sonia isn't right for this job. We need someone Janssen knows and trusts."

"We don't know if Janssen trusts him! And I don't know why you do. Listen, this is not a normal kid, Mikie."

"We don't have time for this discussion—"

"He's got serious problems. Do you even know the first thing about him? Do you know why he was 'emancipated'?"

With a sinking feeling Mikie said, "No, but obviously you do, so enlighten me."

"I pulled his record. His birth mother was a criminal. His first foster family couldn't handle him. Interpersonal problems, lying. The second family paid for judo lessons and private school, and he repays them by beating the crap out of his foster dad. The state concurred with emancipation the minute he turned fifteen. In other words, he was a huge problem child. Yeah, Mikie, this is who you picked to go undercover."

Shit, Mikie thought. Instead she said, "Is that all?"

"'Is that all'? That's not enough?"

She said, "Set up the wire now, please."

"You can't be—"

"I heard you the first time, Wu, and you'll set up the wire or be insubordinate. Then you'll go the hell home and get some sleep. Or do I need to do it myself?"

He did it.

Chapter 36
July 27, 7:30 a.m.

They decided to approach Ty at breakfast. None of them slept in the tense hour that passed after Hal got wired up and coached by the police. Finally, it was time to head to the lodge. Nathan stayed behind with Tanya and Will. Hal was outfitted with a tiny wire that Isaac couldn't see, even though he knew it was there. As they walked to the lodge, Isaac felt strange and unreal. "You look nervous, Isaac," Hal commented. "I expect I should do the talking."

"I'm fine," Isaac said, though he felt queasy and skipped his usual coffee. He managed half a bagel with some cream cheese and strawberries. "But okay, you talk."

Hal appeared completely at ease as he walked over and spoke with Ty. Ty was nodding, agreeing to watch the film. But he looked jumpy, a little annoyed even. His gaze skipped over them and roamed the room; he was probably looking for Nathan.

Maybe we all have secrets, Isaac thought. *But his are ugly.*

They followed Ty down the hall and into his room.

"Let's use your laptop," Hal suggested.

"Nah, I have to update my media player," Ty said. "Use yours."

"I could perform that update for you. It would take a single jiffy."

"No, I have a long to-do list today. But thank you for the offer, my man. Now let's see your work. Your magnum opus, right?"

"We want you to tell us what you think," Isaac said, feeling bold. "Before we show it to the whole camp."

"As I always say, let's roll." He clapped his hands together.

Hal opened his laptop and pressed play.

The scene was familiar—the lake, shimmering under a gray sky—but now it was in black and white, with hazy edges. Nathan had created a silent film, 1920s style. The title appeared on the screen:

A Heritage of Death

"That's fantastic!" Ty said.

"Thank you," Hal said. "Nathan did most of it."

"Where is that kid, anyway?" Ty sounded casual. "Haven't seen him today."

But no one answered. Instead, they watched as pirate Sophie skulked into the frame. She looked left, then right, then tiptoed along the dock.

Where is my minion? the screen read.

A fairy pirate appeared—this was little Eliza, fluttering her wings and dancing down the dock. She ducked into the boathouse and emerged with the clarinet case, then fluttered over to the pirate and handed it over. There was a close-up of Sophie's triumphant face.

AT LAST!!!

"Well done, guys. This is super cool." Ty's tone was dismissive.

"Not quite over, I'm afraid."

The pirate walked over to the dock.

And the ghost of Paul Anderson walked slowly out of the boathouse. He was translucent, shimmering, and dressed all in white.

Isaac watched Ty stop breathing, frozen in his chair.

Sophie jumped into the canoe and began paddling away. Then Isaac appeared onscreen, running down the dock—and right through Paul. The Isaac who stood watching felt a sudden physical chill. He had to stop himself from gasping. There was a quick intake of breath, though, and it came from Ty. His knuckles were white on the arms of his chair. Paul's ghost turned slowly and looked right at them. He took several steps forward, raised his arm, and pointed a finger straight ahead.

"What the fuck?" Ty whispered.

Isaac knew Nathan had done it, but it was still freaking creepy.

Hal was expressionless as he watched Ty, whose attention was glued to the screen, a look of terror on his face.

YOU

Isaac emerged from the water, dripping, towing the canoe. He remembered filming that day—how cold the water had been, how breathtaking Sophie was. Pirate Sophie stomped her foot and handed over the clarinet case.

MY SO-CALLED BROTHER

Ty rolled out of the woods at full speed and handed Isaac a pile of money in exchange for the clarinet case. All this took place on the background of Paul's translucent form, which continued to advance, inexorable, toward the viewer. He turned and pointed a finger at the onscreen Ty. This was where the screen was supposed to say, *It's not what it looks like.* Instead it said,

YOU KILLED ME

"This is not happening, this is not fucking happening," Ty muttered.

CONFESS!!!

And the screen faded to a white mist.

"Well? What do you think?" Hal said brightly.

"What?" Ty said.

"How did you like the film? I know we forgot to include the part about fitting in. We have to add that. But otherwise, it's not bad, is it?"

Isaac had once read a science-fiction story in which robots, given two contradictory orders, would freeze up. All their processing power was diverted to make a decision about what to do, so they couldn't do anything. Ty's face reminded him of one of those robots as he stared at Hal, stymied.

"Do you want to see it again?"

"No. Yes! Yes, show it again."

Isaac thought it was just as spooky the second time around, and he felt the same bizarre chill when he ran through Mai's image onscreen. This time Ty cowered and gasped.

YOU KILLED ME

He slammed the laptop closed. "You're fucking with me," he said. "Aren't you?"

"What do you mean?" Hal asked, all innocence.

Ty's face shone with sweat. There was a harsh smell, suddenly, and Isaac recognized it as fear.

"It wasn't me! I had nothing to do with it, okay?" He was shouting, staring around. Whomever he was talking to, it wasn't them. "Did you see it?"

Hal smiled. It was triumphant, dazzling. "See what, Ty?"

"The—the ghost! Paul—"

Now Hal turned serious. He took Ty's upper arms and got in his face. "What did you do, Ty? What did you do to Paul?"

"Nothing!" Ty cried. "I didn't do anything!"

"You killed him!" Hal shouted. "How did you do it?"

"No! I swear!"

"You gave him peanuts. You fucked with his EpiPen—"

"No! I didn't! Take it—take it away—I can't—" Ty was stammering, pushing the laptop away. Even Hal wasn't quick enough to keep it from hitting the floor with a loud crack.

"Let's go," Hal said, sounding disgusted. They left Ty and went out the door. The detectives and two cops in uniform were running down the hall toward them. Mikie grabbed Hal as the others charged into Ty's room and asked, "Does he have a gun? Any weapon?"

"No, no weapon."

"No weapon!" she shouted at her colleagues' backs. "What was that sound?"

"He broke my computer."

"Are you okay?" They nodded. "Get out of here. Now."

The two boys hurried down the hall and into the cafeteria, where dozens of campers were staring at them. They could just hear Mikie shouting about rights in Ty's room.

They left the lodge and stood on the porch. It was going to be a sunny day.

"Damn it!" Hal said. "It wasn't him."

"But wait!" Isaac cried, chasing after Hal as he speed-walked away from the lodge. "Didn't they tell you it was him? What did you guys talk about at the boathouse?"

"They knew the how, but not the who. Damn! I don't think you should come with me, Isaac. This is going to be dangerous."

So Isaac followed him to the infirmary.

The clamor inside the lodge hadn't yet reached the clinic. Genevieve sat quietly at her desk, a steaming cup of tea in front of her, filling out papers. The scent of Earl Grey reached Isaac's nose, and for a moment he was pierced with sadness, though he didn't know why. "Good morning, guys," she said. Her eyes were light blue, the color of good weather. "Everything all right?"

"Just a quick question," Hal said, closing the door. "Was it the cream pies, or the clarinet?"

"I beg your pardon?"

"I'm thinking clarinet. Maybe the mouthpiece, or even the reed. The cream pie could have gone either way; he might never have been hit with one."

Genevieve looked strange. There was an expression on her face that Isaac couldn't quite identify. When she spoke, her voice was thin and sort of wavery. "Are you feeling okay? Because you're not making any sense."

"I know what happened, Mrs. Rice. And I think I know why. It could have been about the video of Sophie, but I don't think so. No, he wasn't responsible for that."

"What video?" The expression on her face changed. Now that she just looked confused, Isaac recognized what it had been before: she had been afraid.

"Thank you, that makes it a bit clearer," Hal said.

"Makes what clearer? And if you don't mind, I need to open that door," Genevieve said. But she didn't move from her seat.

"Your motivation for killing Paul."

The fear was back now, unmistakable. Isaac felt a pang. *She's always been so kind to me.*

"What?! I have no idea what you're—"

"I assumed it was the baser emotions that led to murder. That was a mistake. To be fair, the detectives made the same error. Thinking someone killed Paul out of hate, or jealousy, or fear. But I'm pretty sure it was love, in your case. You do love Sophie. You were trying to protect her."

Her voice was shrill. "You're completely out of line. You need to leave."

"I don't think you want me to do that, actually." Hal nodded at the window. They could now see the police officers emerging from the lodge. "They're going to figure out they have the wrong person eventually."

Genevieve shook her head emphatically. "You're crazy," she said. "I'm a nurse. I don't kill people, I save them. I tried to save *him*—I gave him the EpiPen, you saw me."

"You gave him insulin. You took out all the epinephrine and replaced it with Sophie's insulin."

She sat down. They watched her shake her head—no, no. But there was no conviction in it. Ty had been frantic to deny his involvement, driven by his terror of ghosts. Genevieve just looked like she had been caught. If Isaac had doubted Hal's conclusion, he didn't any longer. They watched her shake her head.

Genevieve looked at her cup of tea.

"Shall I go on?" Hal said. "I don't mean to upset you, Mrs. Rice."

She looked up and, unexpectedly, she smiled. "Go ahead," she said. "Nothing you say can make any difference now."

Hal said, "I should have put it together sooner! The fire was your attempt to destroy the evidence for what Paul knew: that Sophie was stolen, and that her mother was living in Bangkok, still hoping to find her. He was going to tell her, and you couldn't let that happen."

"You have no idea," she said quietly, "what it's like, raising a child. Maybe you'll do it one day. A child like my daughter, so sensitive, artistic. So lovely, and so...vulnerable. There are things you just can't tell a child like her."

Hal said, "She's seventeen. Not really a child anymore."

She ignored him. "Do you know what happened, after we lost her dad? What we went through? She decided it was her fault. A silly fight they had in the car, over a cell phone! It wasn't enough how badly she was hurt, that she lost her leg...and then she couldn't stop the pain medicine. She nearly killed herself with it, started getting it from some...some dealer!"

"Sophie's stronger than you think," Hal said, but Genevieve wasn't done.

"Then she stopped her insulin for days and days...I can't see her go through that again. I am her mother. Not some Bangkok bar girl who hasn't even seen her since she was born.

"He came to me. Encouraged me to do the 'right thing.'" She laughed without humor. "He said it had been a 'big shock' when he found out, but he said he got over it, and Sophie would too. Got over it! He was about to ruin his life! And that ridiculous therapist thought it was just fine! Abandoning college, leaving his mother and father to join some Buddhist cult in Thailand."

"Buddhism is hardly a—"

She acted like she hadn't even heard him. "As if I would ever let Sophie do such a thing. He said if I didn't tell her, he would. Sophie would have gone into a total tailspin. Back to drugs. Oxy, or something even worse. I would have done anything to prevent that...but it turned out to be so easy." Her gaze was faraway; she almost seemed to be talking to herself.

Hal asked quietly, "How did you do it?"

She startled and looked at him blankly. "It was nothing. Just a little peanut butter on the reed. A little fussing with the EpiPens...I didn't even have to go to the store. When I saw the candy in Tanya's cabin I knew it was meant to be."

"But Mrs. Rice—"

"I know, I know. Look what she's going through now. But he was just another boy. One of many. She'll cry and write a poem, and in ten months she'll graduate and go to college and fall in love with another one. But what he was going to tell her—she never would have gotten over it. I would have lost her again, maybe for good."

"Just another boy," Hal said, and for the first time, he sounded angry.

Then Isaac surprised himself by saying, "It's not only about you. There are other kids just like her. Other mothers."

She shook her head. Her face was completely clear—no guilt, no doubt, no more fear. "I don't care about them," she said. "Only Sophie."

"Mom?" Sophie stood in the doorway between the hallway and the clinic. "What are you talking about?"

"You won't tell," Genevieve said. She looked confident. "You love her too. I know you do. And you, Isaac." She leaned over and reached for their hands, but they both recoiled. "I'm all she has left."

Hal walked out, stopping in the doorway to take Sophie's hand.

"That would be a tragedy," he said, "if it were true."

Chapter 37

July 27, 8:30 p.m.

Mikie was so late for the dinner that it would have been embarrassing to go in, so she sat in her car. She parked a few houses down from her dad's bungalow, and she waited there until the guests were gone. There weren't many. None of them noticed her as they left, and she marveled at how unobservant people were. Her brother emerged, a pretty, red-haired woman at his side—that had to be Melissa—along with Mikie's little nephew, Jack. At eight years old, he worshipped police officers and firefighters. She'd always seen a little bit of herself in Jack: something about the eyes, the way he tilted his head when he was thinking hard. Lately she questioned whether it had all been in her imagination. Who knew what genes they actually shared?

Her dad's lady friend Marie was the last to depart, with a quick kiss at the front door before she drove away in her silver Prius. Mikie liked Marie, who was a retired school principal and had a busy life of her own, but she wasn't ready to pretend everything was the same—not in front of Marie or anyone else. She gave her dad about five minutes before knocking on his door.

He didn't look surprised as he let her in. He looked the same as ever: a trim, dapper man in spectacles, with a neat gray mustache. His shirtsleeves were rolled up to his elbows and he held a dishtowel in his hands, drying them carefully as he closed the door with his elbow. "Case closed?" he asked lightly. "Pour you a drink?"

"Sure."

"No Jamie?"

"Another gig," she said. She'd gone by the bar before coming here, but—lost in the music—he hadn't even seen her, and she'd stayed less than five minutes. She hadn't had a real conversation with him for a couple of days, and she wouldn't tonight either. She was too tired, too disappointed, and she felt too foolish.

"We had pisco sours," her dad said. "Marie's planning a trip to Machu Picchu with her teacher friends." They went into the kitchen, which smelled of lemons and herbs. Plates were already neatly stacked in the dishwasher, and the copper pans were already scrubbed and hanging. Her dad would have cleaned up after himself as he went along, as always. He poured her a frothy drink from the blender. "Need ice?"

"No, thanks. That sounds like a cool trip."

"She loves to travel."

"Too bad you don't." They sat at the breakfast nook. Her dad grew herbs in little terra-cotta pots along the windowsill, just as her mother had.

"Oh, I think she has more fun with her friends anyway. Doesn't mind that I'm a homebody, although she just about has me talked into a trip to Ireland. Wants to explore her roots." He cleared his throat suddenly, as though realizing the pitfalls in what he'd just said. "We missed you tonight."

"My case," she said. "We're about done with it. Thanks for the EpiPen."

"Did it help?"

"It did."

"What was that all about?"

She explained as concisely as she could, but it sounded more convoluted than she'd thought, and took longer to tell: the murder that would have passed for simple anaphylaxis if an ER doc hadn't been bothered by an unexpected lab result, the false trail leading to the camp director, the revelations of child trafficking, and the brother who was injured in a deliberately-set fire then confused matters by using Paul Anderson's insurance card at the emergency room.

"Now why would he do that?" her dad asked.

"No health insurance. He's not an American citizen and he hasn't found work. He's been helping his mother track down a brother he'd never met. And he looked so much like Paul, he was able to use his ID."

He was interested in her work, as he always was—despite his vehement disapproval of her career change at the time. He was astounded that someone had gone to the trouble of sabotaging an EpiPen. As usual, he attributed more of the solve to her than she deserved. "And this was a medical student giving drugs to these kids? And what else, selling papers?"

"Pre-med. He's going to do some serious time, although he probably didn't do the murder..."

"What a reprehensible character."

"He caused a lot of pain, that's for sure." Mikie thought about Katie, who had launched herself at Ty as the officers escorted him to the car. She had shouted at him and slapped his face, just once, before the officers managed to separate them and put her in another car. She sat in the patrol car afterward, dry-eyed and in a kind of daze. Mikie opened the door and sat in the back. "What was that all about?" she asked gently.

"He lied to me," Katie said. "He said Paul had this term paper— and evidence that I'd bought it, and was going to turn me in at college. That Paul was blackmailing Sophie too. And that he was going after me next...and then Sophie gave him the peanuts." She turned to look at Mikie. "She didn't though, did she?"

"It doesn't look that way. Was it you who sent the fax?"

Katie nodded.

"Why?" Mikie thought she understood. "To get Sophie in trouble?"

"Not only that. It was just..." Katie sighed. "Everyone thought he was perfect, and I thought he was being so cruel...and that he had everyone fooled...but it wasn't Paul, was it? It was Ty, all along." She covered her face with her hands. "I'm so dumb."

"Ty tricked a lot of people," Mikie said. "Doesn't make you dumb."

"Paul was my friend," she said. "I should have known."

"He sounds like a good guy."

"You know what's weird?" She sat up and looked at Mikie. "I actually feel better. Ty's a jerk, but Paul was good. He was. I started to think nobody was. Even though he's dead, I'm glad I know better now."

Now Mikie's father was asking, "But how on earth did you put it all together?"

"I didn't." She sighed. "I got it wrong. A teenager figured it out, a computer hacker. Strange kid, but very smart." Hal Shaw was still a mystery. She wondered how much of what Wu said about him was true, and, if it was, how he'd managed to come so far. "We have the nurse in custody now, we even have a confession, but I'm not sure the case will hold up."

"Why not?"

"No physical evidence. We don't have the EpiPen. We don't have the reed with the peanut butter on it. If she threw them in the lake, chances are we'll never find them."

"Can't you drag the lake?"

"Not for something that small. There were so many prints on the peanut butter cup wrapper that it's useless, even if having the candy proved anything, which it doesn't. She admitted everything to a teenager while we were busy arresting someone else. He got it on tape but

I'm not sure it's admissible because he was mic'd for the other suspect…and it wasn't exactly regulation." She gritted her teeth, wishing Hal had waited for her.

"But it all sounds so plausible. She had motive and opportunity."

Mikie smiled to herself. Her dad loved detective novels and *Mystery!* on PBS. "Yup. And most importantly, she did give him a shot. Plenty of witnesses to that. So you never know. But if it does go to trial, the defense will say he might just as easily have killed himself. Hard to prove he didn't know he was giving himself insulin."

"Surely that's not reasonable."

"We actually thought he might have committed suicide at one point, so it's not as crazy as it sounds."

"Why, because of the life insurance?"

"That and the will." Her dad said nothing. The word "will" sat heavily on the counter before them, an invisible weight that they both looked at for a moment.

"Mikie, about that will," her dad started. He cleared his throat again. "Believe me, I had no idea the man had anything like that planned. If I had known…"

"I'm not angry, Dad."

He let out a big breath. "Thank God," he said.

"Which is not to say I don't think you should've said something earlier. And Mom."

"You're right, of course."

"I mean, I believed a lie all these years."

"But it wasn't a lie," he said. "Not in a way that matters. I'm your dad, Mikie, even if you don't carry my genes."

"I know, Dad." And she did. She'd seen Mr. Anderson, whose grief was every bit as real as that of any bereaved parent. She'd seen Genevieve Rice and the twisted motherlove that made her so possessive and protective that it had driven her to murder. "But it would have been nice to know before now."

"I can see that."

"There may be family history considerations."

"Okay, we can look into that if you want."

"Plus, I could have looked forward to this inheritance." He eyed her warily, and she grinned. "Just kidding." They drank their pisco sours peacefully for a minute. She wanted to ask how he'd forgiven her mother, but she thought better of it. That part wasn't important anymore. Maybe he'd needed forgiveness too. Maybe everyone did, from time to time.

Chapter 38

July 28, 10:00 a.m.

Isaac had about an hour. His parents were coming; everyone's parents were coming. In the fallout of the murder and ensuing scandal, camp was effectively over, and there was something he had to do. Hal had already run his face through the program and assured him: "You're not related to Sophie. At least not closely."

"Are you sure?" Isaac wondered how he could see anything with the laptop screen cracked and screwed up. Fortunately, the hard drive wasn't affected.

"I'm positive. And Isaac—I didn't tell Sophie this, but it looks like she and Paul might have been."

"Might have been what?" Then he realized. "Oh!" That would be awkward.

"Probably best not to mention that. I'll talk to her about it later."

"Wait. Do you think—" Isaac started, but Hal had read his mind. "Yes," he said. "I think Paul knew."

Isaac found Sophie at the boathouse, staring into the water. She was holding a bunch of orange fabric in her lap.

"Hi," he said.

"Don't," she said. "I'm so embarrassed."

"Why?"

"Just—everything."

"Don't be embarrassed," Isaac said, which seemed horribly inadequate. She rolled her eyes and went back to looking at the water. He nodded at the bundle she was holding. "What's that?"

"Robes," she said.

They looked familiar somehow. "Wait, are those...monk robes?"

She nodded, holding them tightly. "I know I should give them to his parents, but I don't want to. They didn't know he was going. They would have hated it. They might throw them away or something."

"Wait, what? Paul was going to be a monk?"

"Just for a year," she said. "He said it was a Thai thing. He was 'making merit,' trying to make up for some things he'd done that he wished he hadn't. And he was becoming a Buddhist. Thinking about it, anyway. I didn't want him to go. But now I wish he had." He couldn't think of anything to say. She looked up at him and smiled. "I kind of feel like maybe he did go. Maybe he's there now, instead of..."

"Yeah," Isaac said. "Maybe."

"I took his passport, too," she said. She opened it and they looked at his picture. He had a good face, and it was a nice picture. He hadn't smiled, but he looked happy. "I figured if I had his robes and passport, then he couldn't go. Stupid."

"It's not stupid. Maybe you should just keep those things."

"You know what? I'm totally keeping them. I'm going to live with my grandparents and they won't mind. They won't even ask."

"Why are you going to live with them?"

She looked hard at him. "Do you really think I want to live with her? After what she did? There's no way. Even if she doesn't go to prison."

It was hard to know what to say to that, so Isaac just sat with her.

"I don't really want her to, though," Sophie said eventually. Her voice was very soft. "I mean...I don't know. She's still my mom, you know? But I'd rather live with my grandparents for now."

Isaac asked, "Where do they live?"

"Waldport. Why?"

Isaac took a deep breath. "I was just hoping that we could keep in touch. Because I like you."

Her eyes were brown today, and they looked real. She looked completely baffled. "Why would you say that?" she said. "When I'm this crazy person. This—idiot. With a crazy mother."

"Your mom's not your fault. And you're not crazy."

"You don't know half of it. I like you too, Isaac. A lot. But I'm a mess, really. And I'm not...not over Paul. You should find a normal girl."

"Sophie, look. I know a lot—"

"Oh, God, I hope not," she said and buried her face in handfuls of saffron fabric.

"But I do. I didn't mean to. Things just sort of came out, and I'm sorry. I know more about you than you know about me, and none of it matters to me, but it doesn't seem fair." She looked at him then. "I wanted to tell you—well, it's easier if I just show you. I'm not exactly normal, myself." Isaac took out his wallet. His hands, to his surprise, were steady. He unfolded the glossy photo that Ty had shown him the other day, wielding it like a weapon that said, *I know who you are.* It was a photo of all the Heritage campers from two years earlier, lined up on the quad in their T-shirts. Ty had circled Isaac's face with a marker, so there was no hiding. It was hard for him to look at it, but she took it and studied the page like it was no big deal.

"When is this from? Three years ago?"

"Year before last." His voice was hoarse, and he cleared his throat.

"Wow," she said. "Look at my hair. Bad."

He tried to laugh. It came out false, a croak. "That's nothing next to mine."

"I thought you were new."

He took a deep breath. "In a way," he said, "I am." His hands trembled, but he took her hand and guided her index finger to the spot. He had stood cringing in the middle row, trying to be invisible, a feat that was hampered by a puffy halo of permed hair—and now even more by the circle Ty had drawn. "Isaac Whitson hasn't ever been to camp."

"Well, who is that?"

His heart pounded. It was so hard to say the name. It had been months since he'd done so. A simple thing, but it actually hurt. He felt like his chest would split right down the middle if she started using that name—but she wouldn't. He had to believe she wouldn't. And if she did? He would walk away, or jump into the lake, or just die on the spot.

But he didn't have to say it after all.

"Oh!" she said. "I remember her." And then she said nothing, only looked down at the photo. Neither of them said anything. Isaac heard some kids across the lake yelling, the whine of a mosquito, the water slapping the pylons. He counted to ten, then to twenty. *Oh well*, he thought. *Michelle will be proud of me. I was brave.* He braced his hands at his sides and stood up to go. Sophie didn't move.

"Anyway. I just wanted to say that," he said. "And, um, have a good rest of your summer."

"I mean," she said quietly, "I remember *you*."

"Yeah," he said. And then there didn't seem to be anything more to say. He turned to go.

"Wait," she said. "Was I...mean?"

"What?"

"To you. Back then. Was I kind of a bitch? I could be. I mean, I can be. I don't exactly remember."

"No. You weren't mean."

"I'm glad," she said. "Sit back down." He did. She leaned over and unbuckled her prosthesis. "Look at this," she said firmly. She pulled her pant leg up to reveal the spot where her skin ended. The skin was smooth, but the surface was bumpy and pink. It looked like a landscape of some kind, unusual, but not ugly. She took his hand and touched it to the warm skin there. It just felt like skin—maybe a bit knobby underneath, like a knee. "We're even," she said.

"Okay." His relief was enormous, bigger than trees, bigger than sequoias even. They sat quietly for a few minutes. He moved his hand to hers, and they sat touching that way, looking at the water until it was time to go.

Notes on International Adoption

This book is a work of fiction, inspired—like most fiction—by the real world. However, no real people are portrayed in the book, which is entirely a product of my (overactive) imagination. Any resemblance of a given character to a living person is a coincidence.

International adoption is a complicated issue, and people have intense feelings about it. Most adoptive families are a lot like birth families: they have good days and bad days—and days when family members find one another very aggravating! Some adoptees deeply resent the process that uprooted them from their culture as babies and, as adults, come to oppose international adoption as a false solution to the economic and social problems that lead to child abandonment in the sending countries. Others express gratitude to their adoptive parents for giving them a better life. I can't speak for adoptees, of course, but my sense from talking to many is that most fall somewhere between these two points of view. It is true that kids do better in foster and adoptive families than they do in institutions such as orphanages, where many children languish when there is no social safety net. It is also true that every international adoption starts from a place of sadness and primal loss with the separation of a parent and child. If we ignore either of these issues, we do a disservice to every member of the adoption triad: birth parent, child, and adoptive parent.

As an adoptive mom myself, I am endlessly grateful for my children and the agency that brought us together (Holt International Children's Services, which truly is ethical and child centered). It would be impossible for me to convey the gratitude I feel toward the women who gave birth to my children and toward the foster families who cared for them before I did. Yet adoption only happens when something tragic has occurred: a child losing their birth family because of death, severe poverty, illness, or abuse. Most adoptive families don't want to even consider the possibility that crime and corruption could be part of the process, but it has happened. The Hague Adoption Convention, mentioned in the book, is both real and necessary.

Heritage Camp is not a real location. Some readers may recognize features of Holt Adoptee Camp. I am a huge fan of Holt Camp! If you know an adoptee between ages nine and eighteen, please encourage their participation in any of the sessions that take place around the US every summer. Rest assured—in several seasons as the camp nurse, I have never seen any of the teenaged shenanigans described in this book. The kids are fantastic, the counselors (all adoptees) are awesome, and the directors have been caring, competent, and nothing at all like Ty Janssen.

Acknowledgments

Thank you to my parents, who filled our home with books, and my sister, the writer E.C. Hanlon, who showed me it could be done.

Thank you to my first readers, especially Benjamin Chambers and Delona Campos-Davis, both terrific writers. Many thanks to my book club for the years of friendship and encouragement. I am especially grateful to Kendra Kaiser, recently retired from the Oregon State Police, who provided details about police procedures in the event of an unexpected death. Any errors in that department are mine, not hers. Thank you to Tom, my favorite husband, whose hard work in Ontario, Canada, from 2014 to 2015 allowed me to take a writing sabbatical. Thank you, Ottawa, for being so cold that I had no choice but to stay in and write all winter, yet also for providing such a warm welcome. The Ottawa Public Library provided everything a fledgling writer could need: a writers' group (run by the fabulous middle grade/YA author Michael Stewart), space for NaNoWriMo participants, and even a mystery workshop with Barbara Fradkin (check out the Inspector Green series) and a very useful talk by Maureen Jennings (Detective Murdoch and more). I must also thank my coworkers and employers at Columbia River Women's Center for allowing me to take a year off (and letting me come back!). You all rock!

My deepest appreciation to the folks at Ooligan Press who plucked my manuscript from the e-shelves and helped me polish it into a novel I can be proud of. Many publishing students provided sensitivity readings, suggestions, and careful line editing, and while I don't know the names of all these individuals, I am grateful to each one of them. Erica Wright, Olivia Rollins, Dani Nicholson, Abbey Gaterud, and Bailey Potter kept me A: calm, and B: not quite so calm that I stopped working. Bless you all!

And most of all, thank you to Harry, Theo, and Betty. If you hadn't granted me the title, I wouldn't be a mom. And that's my favorite job.

About the Author

Jennifer Hanlon Wilde lives and writes in Oregon. She is a nurse practitioner and teacher who thinks of her work as opening a kind of map to study the well-worn places where storytelling intersects with health. She also enjoys real maps, traveling the world with her family, and, as a doctoral student at Washington State University, nerding out over global health data. A robust community theater and music scene, acres of orchards, and unparalleled local cider and beer have made it a joy for her to put roots down in the Columbia River Gorge, but being a Boston Red Sox fan is in her DNA. This is her first novel.

Ooligan Press

Ooligan Press is a student-run publishing house rooted in the rich literary culture of the Pacific Northwest. Founded in 2001 as part of Portland State University's Department of English, Ooligan is dedicated to the art and craft of publishing. Students pursuing master's degrees in book publishing staff the press in an apprenticeship program under the guidance of a core faculty of publishing professionals.

Project Managers
Dani Nicholson
Bailey Potter

Editing
Olivia Rollins
Erica Wright

Design
Denise Morales Soto
Morgan Ramsey

Digital
Megan Crayne
Chris Leal

Marketing
Sydnee Chelsey
Hannah Boettcher

Publicity
Alexandria Gonzales

Social Media
Faith Muñoz
Alix Martinez

Book Production
Jenna Amundson
Cole Bowman
Alex Burns
Sophie Concannon
Melinda Crouchley
Jenny Davis
Scott Fortmann
Amanda Fink
Katherine Flitsch
Rebecca Gordon
Grace Hansen
Rachel Howe
Elle Klock
Jennifer Ladwig
Rachel Lantz
Stephanie Johnson
  Lawson

Nif Lindsay
Archer Long
Kaylee Lovato
Rosina Miranda
Vivian Nguyen
Claire Plaster
Luis Ramos
Rachael Renz
Riley Robert
Shalyn Schipper
Kaitlyn Shehee
Tia Sprague
Emma St. John
Xian Wang
Rylee Warner
Mary Williams
Courtney Young
Kelly Zatlin